GOIN'
COASTAL

GOIN' COASTAL

Four Cozy Mysteries
Set Along the Shore

Jayne Ormerod

BAY BREEZE PUBLISHING, LLC ◆ NORFOLK, VA

GOIN' COASTAL
Four Cozy Mysteries Set Along the Shore

Goin' Coastal is comprised of the following stories:
- "Home is Where You Hang Your Flip Flops"
- "Down by the Bay" (Originally published as "Behind the Blue Door: 230 Periwinkle Place", Bay Breeze Publishing, 2014, now with remastered "cozier" ending.)
- "Seas the Day"
- "The Tide Also Rises", (Originally published in *Chesapeake Crimes 3*, Wildside Press, 2008, now with a remastered, "cozier" ending.

Cover Design by San Coils at CoverKicks.com

ISBN: ISBN-13: 978-1-7327907-1-1
ISBN-10: 1-7327907-1-X

Published by
Bay Breeze Publishing, LLC
Norfolk, VA

TABLE OF CONTENTS

HOME IS WHERE YOU HANG YOUR FLIP FLOPS

Meet Sydney Taveras, a middle-aged woman who is reinventing herself after a messy divorce. Based on Internet pictures alone, she rents a pink cottage on the Chesapeake Bay. Before the healing process begins, she is drawn into a decades-old mystery when her new neighbor admits to having killed a man. The question is whom did she kill? And perhaps more importantly, where did she hide the body?

CHAPTER ONE

Life lesson number 313...
Never rent a house based on Internet pictures.

It was ten o'clock on a sunny September morning as I steered my trusty old 4Runner to the curb in front of 790 Waters Edge Circle in Norfolk, Virginia. This was a milestone moment for me, as I'd left my old life—specifically my old ex-husband—behind to embark on a new one of tranquility and reflection. I'd packed the bare necessities of life, to include my kitchen gadgets and ten boxes of my favorite books. (Cooking and reading are my two passions in life.) At the last minute I had the presence of mind to throw in an air mattress, along with a card table and two metal chairs. Everything else I would purchase new. New life, new stuff, new me. That was the plan, anyway.

Based on Internet pictures alone, I'd rented a home on the shores of the Chesapeake Bay, an oh-*sooooo*-cute pink cottage with gingerbread trim, and a deep front porch just made for sitting. But one glance around my new neighborhood and I understood why, despite the to-die-for HGTV interior, it had sat vacant for seven months. The surrounding neighborhood consisted of a narrow, crumbling asphalt road that meandered through a cluster of about two dozen abandoned WWII bungalows. Their small yards were mostly sand dotted with overgrown weeds. Every window was cracked or broken, and shutters either lay on the ground, hung dejectedly from rusty hooks, or were missing entirely. None of the homes had seen the business end of a paint brush in probably half a century. I refused to allow myself to even think about what assortment of creatures dwelled within.

The street T-boned at a sand dune. I knew from studying the map of my new neighborhood that the Chesapeake Bay waited on the other side for me, but I probably could have figured that out based on the salty scent blowing in on the breeze.

I drove along the bumpy lane looking for signs of life in the dilapidated houses. The last one on my right had hope, if the sturdy white-picket fence was any indication. Another good sign—a neatly tended raised vegetable garden filled the backyard. Mostly tomatoes supported by cages, and pole beans climbing up kite string. The house itself had all its shutters (another good sign) but they, like the clapboard exterior, suffered a severe case of paint-fade. My guess was the house had once been a peachy color with black shutters, but was now barely beige with chalky grey trim. But what really made it stand out against all the other homes was the freshly painted front door. Bright blue. Cerulean, if I remembered my Crayola crayon colors correctly.

The door was cracked open and I saw a shadow behind. Someone was watching me.

I waved.

The door slammed shut.

Despite being hemmed in by houses, I had never felt so alone in all my life.

* * * * * *

Two hours later, while sitting in my truck parked in front of the little pink cottage, I made a phone call. My best friend back in Ohio answered her phone on the first ring. "Sydney?"

"Hey, Tasha."

"You've been crying," she said. Yeah, we knew each other that well. "Are you okay? Did your truck break down? Did you eat bad barbecue on the road? Or do you just miss me that much?"

Despite my best efforts, the tears gushed again.

"Tell me where you are. I'll book a flight and be there by nightfall."

That made me cry harder. I suddenly missed my friend, my home, and the life I'd left behind. So much for a fresh start. My ex had told me I wasn't the adventurous type, and I so wanted to prove him wrong.

Tasha stayed on the phone until I got my emotions in check and I'd told her the entire story.

"Is it as close to the beach as promised?"

"Half of a block." I fingered the keychain Tasha had given me as a going away present, a pair of conjoined flip-flops imprinted with the phrase "Home is where you Hang your Flip Flops." I smiled through my tears. This is what I wanted, what I'd dreamed of doing. I couldn't quit now. Not yet.

"What's the area around that neighborhood like?"

After the blue door had shut me—and my inquisitive eyes—out, I'd turned my truck around and driven aimlessly for two hours. First pointing my 4Runner west towards the interstate then circling back east to the little pink cottage by the sea. I traveled east-west-east-west, screaming at myself at every U-turn. I'd added a little south-north direction for variety, but soon figured out the further away I drove from the shore, the more derelict the neighborhoods became. For the most part, the houses on the water were impressive. I'd parked and walked a few miles on the beach, letting the sound of the gentle surf and the warm breezes sooth my troubled soul. That was when I realized this is where I was meant to be right now.

"There are some McMansions on the Bay," I told Tasha. "And across the street are some okay houses but lots of run-down shacks that could be flop houses or meth labs. Lots of new construction, so the area seems to be in transition. I gotta tell you, I've never seen such a mish-mash of good and bad all snuggled up together like this."

"McMansions are a good sign," Tasha said. "More appealing to thieves than your place. So you should be safe. Remember why you moved there, so you could take long walks on the beach and spend time getting to know yourself again. That you can still do. Then at night you bolt your front door and curl up on the sofa and watch old movies. I envy you the solitude." She had a wistful note in her voice.

I imagine my situation did look good compared to the three-ring circus she ran with four kiddos under the age of ten.

"What you need to do is bake a batch of your wonderful triple-chocolate cupcakes, and then march down and introduce yourself to your new neighbor. You'll feel better after that."

Trust Tasha to give me a workable plan of action.

"But you better not find a new best friend down there. That's my job, and I'm not giving it up without a fight."

"You're my best friend forever," I promised, then disconnected.

I had the truck unloaded in under an hour. Shopping for coastal décor would commence first thing tomorrow morning.

Having settled in, I made a quick trip to a grocery store to purchase all the implements for baking. Then I headed back to my little pink cottage (which was every bit as charming as the Internet photos) and whipped up a batch of triple-chocolate cupcakes with chocolate fudge frosting.

I felt better already, proof once again that chocolate is the cure for just about everything.

* * * * * *

Hi. My name is Sydney Taveras."

The cerulean-blue door that had cracked open at my knock didn't slam in my face. I thought it a good sign and continued speaking. "I just moved into the pink house down the street. I baked these cupcakes today and no way can I eat them all myself so I thought I'd share, and maybe pick your brain about good places to eat and shop around here."

The door opened a little further and revealed a small, older woman. She may have been five-feet four-inches tall, if she weren't so stopped over. She had curly, blue-rinsed hair and was dressed in a pale-yellow, seersucker housedress. Scrawny legs stuck out below the ragged hem and her feet were stuffed into grungy slippers that at one point in their life might—or might not—have been dolphins. When she lifted her head and looked at me, I saw small eyes set deep in ash-gray skin. Her gaze flitted to the plate of cupcakes then back to my face.

"What kind of cupcakes?" she asked, her voice raspy, as if she'd smoked all her life.

"Chocolate."

The door swung open. "C'mon in. My name's Alva Rose Llewellyn."

I stepped inside the dark room which was small and cluttered with lots of furniture but somehow managed to maintain an orderly feel. The smell of damp dog permeated the air, although I didn't see any signs of a canine companion, wet or dry.

"I'll get some napkins," she said. "Make yourself comfortable."

With a choice between an old orange sofa and a brown, faux-leather recliner, neither of which appeared to have much stuffing left inside, I opted for the recliner. After setting the plate of cupcakes on the warped and dated fanzines that filled every inch of the coffee table, I settled back in the chair,

Alva Rose shuffled back in with a stack of white paper napkins, the fancy kind my mother used when the garden club came to luncheon. She helped herself to a cupcake, pulled off the paper wrapper and ate it in three bites. She reached for another one. "These are good," she said around a mouthful of chocolate.

"Thank you."

"Can't tell you the last time I had a cupcake this good. I don't do much fancy cooking any more. No one to enjoy it, not since Rusty, that's my son, moved out."

"Oh," I said, unable to tell by her voice or body language if that had been a good thing he'd moved out (like he'd grown up and got married) or a bad thing, (like he'd gone to jail.)

She worked her way through two more cupcakes before speaking again. "I used to make the best fudge. Rusty loved it. He had quite a sweet tooth, that boy. He was a mechanic down at the Lube 'N Oil and lived in the back bedroom and did stuff around the house for me. We got along well and all." She paused to lick a bit of chocolate off the outside edge of her hand. "But that all changed the day I killed a man."

CHAPTER TWO

I raced back to my little pink cottage as fast as my flip-flopped feet would carry me, hitting the speed dial for Tasha before I was through the front door. "Ohmygawd. Ohmygawd. Ohmygawd," I said, but it came out more like a hysterical whimper.

"Sydney," Tasha said, "you are going to have to calm down and tell me what's happened or I can't help you." She was her usual unruffled self, and had rightly pegged me as smack dab in the middle of an emotional tailspin.

"I'll call you back." I disconnected, braced my hands on the counter, leaned forward and drew in a deep breath. Then another. And another. Realizing that those childbirth breathing techniques were no more effective on a murder-confession-induced panic attack than they had been when I'd delivered any of my three sons, I gave up and went for the chocolate cupcakes. It took two, with a merlot chaser, before I'd calmed down enough to call Tasha back.

"What's up, honey?" she asked.

"My new neighbor admitted to me that she killed a man."

"When?"

"I don't know."

"Why?"

"I don't know."

"Was it an accident?"

"I don't know." I felt a pattern developing to my answers, and realized how foolish I was being.

"Was it self-defense? 'Cuz that would make it an okay

9

thing."

"Yeah, I guess it would. But I don't know."

"What *do* you know?"

"That she told me her son moved out the day she killed a man."

"Did she say it in a cold-blooded killer kind of way?"

"No." I thought about it for a minute. "More matter-of-fact kind of way."

"Honey, I think we're gonna need a little more information. You might be overreacting just the teensiest bit here."

I poured myself another merlot. Overreacting was not in my nature. But picking up and moving 1,223 miles away from the people I loved and knew were *not* killers was not in my nature either.

Tasha and I chatted a few more minutes. I laughed to the point of snorting as she regaled me with the tale of her six-year-old twin boys latest "art project"—graffiti-ing the kitchen's biscuit-colored walls with hot fudge they'd found in the fridge. She'd run to the restroom and had been gone three minutes, tops. Those boys have a nose for mischief.

Before we hung up, Tasha gave me a productive plan of action. "You do some Googling and I bet you find out there's a good reason for Alva Rose to have killed that man," she said. "*If* she did. The only thing she might be guilty of is having a vivid imagination."

More active than mine right now? Impossible.

"You be careful, you hear?" Tasha said. "Lock your door and keep your pepper spray near."

Oh, yeah. That. I'd meant to pick some up while out this afternoon, but I'd been more concerned with baking cupcakes than my personal safety. Chocolate can be so distracting.

"Tell me you bought some pepper spray today," Tasha said, using the same voice she used on her twins.

"I could tell you I did, but I'd be lying, and you'd know it." I lifted my finger to my mouth and started nibbling on my nail. Then remembered the new and improved Sydney

Taveras didn't nibble on fingernails. I tucked my hand in the pocket of my shorts, safely away from my nibbling habits.

"I'm not going to sleep a wink tonight, thinking of an unarmed BFF sleeping alone in a sketchy neighborhood," Tasha said. "You call me if there's any sign of trouble." She paused for a moment. "Well, call nine-one-one first, then call me."

"Okay."

"And call me first thing in the morning so I know you survived the night."

"Will do."

"I miss you, Syd. Sending hugs through the phone."

"Miss you too, Tash. Goodbye." I hit the END button on my phone before she had to listen to another round of tears from me. I'd only cried once in the past three years, on the occasion of my divorce being final. Tears twice in one day today was a personal best, and not something I was very proud of.

A half of a box of Kleenex later, my tears had slowed to an occasional, annoying drip. Time to get to work.

I pulled out my brand-new tablet—a gift to myself so I could watch old movies while alone at night—and Googled the heck out of Alva Rose Llewellyn of Norfolk, Virginia.

I learned that Llewellyn is of Welsh origin.

I found there is a Llewellyn Avenue in Norfolk.

I waded through the information regarding a John William Llewellyn who'd lived here in the 1700s, but couldn't find a connection between the street and the man (or his heirs), and no connection what-so-ever to Alva Rose.

I linked through to see that Thomas Alva Edison (of phone-invention fame) lived in a home called Glenmont in the historic neighborhood of Llewellyn Park.

Next thing I knew I was watching baby pygmy goat videos (I still don't know how that happened . . .)

At midnight I gave up, having not found a single

mention of Alva Rose Llewellyn anywhere in the whole of cyberspace. Odd, that, for if she'd killed a man certainly there'd be some mention of it in some paper somewhere in the world.

But I had only scratched the tip of the iceberg, as there were other ways to spell her last name, like Llywelyn or Llewelyn.

A thought crossed my mind. *Was Alva Rose Llewellyn even her real name?*

Things were getting complicated. I'd think better on a rested mind. It had been a physically, mentally, emotionally and spiritually exhausting day.

After shutting the tablet down, I got ready for bed, all the time my mind fabricating wild and wacky scenarios as to why Alva Rose had told me she'd killed a man.

My first night in my new home would be spent on an air mattress on the floor of the family room. The upstairs bedroom tucked under a gabled roof was super charming, but every slight noise echoed in the cavernous space. Footsteps sounded like thunderclaps. Even my breathing echoed off the walls and ceiling and it sounded like Darth Vader was in the room with me. No thanks! Too spooky and isolated.

I curled up, pulled my new soft blanket over my head (baby pink, a color my ex hated and refused to let into the house), and counted the ways a person could kill a man and get away with it.

It was three a.m. before I fell into a restless sleep.

CHAPTER THREE

BAM! BAM! BAM!

The sound had me sitting up on the air mattress, pink blanket tucked under my chin, wondering what the hell was going on. I was too pissed to be scared.

Then a voice, muffled, came through the door. "Ms. Taveras. Ms. Sydney Taveras. I'm a Norfolk police officer and I need you to come to the door."

Oh, for gawd's sake. What could the police possibly want at this ungodly hour of the morning?

Wait . . . maybe it was a ruse to get me to the door where some bad guys would force themselves past me and steal all my worldly belongings? Or worse?

BAM! BAM! BAM! "Police. Please open your door."

My heart hammered in my chest and my knees were as wobbly as a new foal's as I hauled myself up off the air mattress. Wrapped in my blanket, I shuffled to the front entrance. It was then I realized the thick steel door had no peephole, nor did it have cute windows on each side with which to look out and see whether the person on the other side was friend or foe.

BAM! BAM! BAM!

I jumped at the sound. This person meant business. And he must be legit because what kind of bad person knocks on the door? Trouble prefers entering unannounced via a broken window.

I drew a deep breath and opened the door just a crack. I blinked against the bright sunshine before focusing on one of Norfolk's finest, dressed in blue and with all the implements of crime-fighting strapped to his belt. The gun drew my attention. Even holstered, that thing scared the beejezus out of me.

"Are you Sydney Taveras?" he asked.

I lifted my gaze from the gun to his face. "Yes." Thinking about that Glock on his hip, I quickly added, "Sir."

He slipped his hands so that they rested on his weapons, squared his shoulders and said, "I'll need to see some identification, please."

"What's this all about?"

"Identification please."

"Okay." I shut the door and slipped the deadbolt, leaving the officer standing on the front porch while I went in search for my purse. Finding the almost-suitcase-sized duffle in a kitchen cabinet where I'd shoved it for safe keeping until I got organized, I dug through the mess of papers, newly acquired beach necessities and things I wanted to find easily during the move (like my phone-charging equipment and a selection of corkscrews.) Eventually my hand wrapped around my wallet and I pulled out my Ohio driver's license.

Back at the front door I handed over my ID. He looked at it, then at me, then at the license, and then at me. I will admit, I didn't look much like that picture, not since Tasha had treated me to a total makeover after my ex moved out. No more waist-length gray hair pulled into a ponytail. After a short, fashionable cut and color change to dusty blond, I looked more like the mid-40s Heidi Klum than the aging Roseanne Barr my license picture resembled.

"It's me," I offered. "That was taken before my transformation to *Gay Divorcee*."

He looked at me kind of funny. I get that a lot when I quote old movie titles or bits of dialogue.

"I mean 'gay' in the happy kind of way. It's an old Fred Astaire, Ginger Rogers movie."

He looked at my license again then back at me.

Apparently satisfied, he handed it back.

"Now can you tell me what this is about?" I asked.

"Your sister called the station."

"I don't—"

"Name of," he pulled a memo book out of his shirt pocket and flipped through a few pages, "Tasha Kerns."

"Oh, that sister," I said, smiling. That's not a total lie. We were *practically* sisters.

"She reported that she has been calling you every ten minutes since six this morning and you have not answered. She asked us to come check on you."

"What time is it now?"

"A quarter past eleven."

"What?" I hadn't slept that late in over forty years! And Tasha knew it. Poor Tasha. She had to be worried sick. "I'm fine, as you can see. I'll call her right away."

"If you're sure you're okay, then I'll be on my way."

"Thank you so much, Officer . . ." I read his nametag . . . "Grant."

I started to shut the door, then a thought occurred to me. Seemed like Officer Grant might be able to help me with my search for the truth in the Alva Rose Llewellyn situation. I called after him. "I do have a question, if you have a moment."

He turned.

I tried to smile, but I fear I only accomplished a sickly grimace. "If someone casually mentioned to a person—not me, though, this is a question for a friend—and it's kind of weird but a total stranger told my friend that she killed a man. Would I, I mean my friend, be required to tell the police?"

His eyes narrowed, ever-so accusingly.

"It's not me. I swear. And it's not even real." I drew a deep sigh and channeled my inner Barbara Stanwyck. "It's for a story I'm writing. I just moved here from Ohio, and I'm hoping the beach atmosphere will get my creative juices flowing and I'll write the next blockbuster mystery." I have no earthly idea where that fabrication came from, but it seemed to work.

Officer Grant smiled. Quite charmingly, I might add, and his aggressive body language throttled back about six clicks. "We get a lot of mystery writers around here. In fact, there's a chapter of them meets down at the Greenbriar Library. I spoke at one of their meetings a few months ago. You might want to check them out."

"I will."

"But to answer your question, we would need a little more information to go on. And it certainly helps if we have a dead body. People make false statements all the time, usually to get street cred in gangs and things. Is your character a gangbanger?"

An image of scrawny old Alva Rose as a gangbanger almost made me laugh. But it did occur to me she might be trying to earn some street cred herself, in a way, with me. Maybe to lead me to believe if I tried to rob her or something, she wouldn't hesitate to kill me, too. "Yeah, kind of."

"If there's no real crime, your character has nothing to worry about. But if there's proof that a murder occurred, and it is discovered that the person confessed to didn't report it, then that person could be charged as an accessory after the fact. That'll earn you a few years in jail, maybe less, depending on how good a lawyer you have."

"Oh, okay. Good to know. Thank you so much."

Officer Grant pulled a business card out of his front shirt pocket and handed it to me. "If you have any other questions, just give a call. I've taken it as my personal mission to get police procedures reflected correctly in books, and especially on TV. Like a DNA test is gonna come back in a day." He snorted. "Give me a break."

"Yeah, I know. Unbelievable." I rolled my eyes in affinity, although I don't watch any of the current cable line-up. I'm more of an historical romance reader than contemporary mystery, so didn't know if the writers got it wrong or right. I'd need to study the genre if I was going to write something. And, truth be told, the idea intrigued me.

I took the card and thanked him.

He left.

I stood on the front step, looking out towards the bay beyond the dunes, and gave serious thought to what Officer Grant had told me.

Jail. Hmm. I didn't like the sound of that. Not one little bit. I'd seen the 1950s movie *Caged* staring Eleanor Parker and Agnes Morehead, and had no desire to rub elbows with hardened criminals.

As I gazed off towards the beach, I set a new goal for my first day of my new life in Norfolk, Virginia—keep my rear end out of hoosegow!

You'd think that would be easy enough to do.

CHAPTER FOUR

After finding my cell phone—tucked in the same drawer as my purse, which explains why I hadn't heard it ring—I saw I had twenty-six missed calls from Tasha. I called her back.

"Are you okay?" She sounded breathless, which I translated to worried sick.

"I'm fine. Just overslept. Must be all this sea air."

"I was about to book a plane ticket."

"No need. I'm fine. Really."

"Thank goodness." She drew a deep breath. In the background I heard a tremendous crash, followed by a scream. "Damn it. Twin trouble. I gotta run."

"Hope they're okay."

"I'm sure it's nothing a trip to the ER won't take care of."

We said a quick goodbye, and ended the call.

Gawd, I missed that woman.

I had an entire day ahead of me. I'd planned to do some shopping to outfit my cottage, but before I could Google coastal décor stores, my gaze caught the sunlight and seagrass outside my window. Forget shopping. What I needed was a long walk on the beach. I changed into a pair of navy capris and an oversized white button-down shirt, slipped on a well-worn pair of Sanuks and was out the door in three minutes flat.

The public beach access ran next to Alva Rose's house. I headed down the street at a brisk pace. I needed to clear my head and set some goals for my new life. I did like the idea of writing a novel, one with a little murder in it might be interesting. Might be therapeutic to kill off my ex and his new wife, in the literary sense, that is.

I crested the dunes. The view took my breath away. Smooth water as far as the eye could see before it dipped off over the horizon. A tanker and some sort of gray, U.S. Navy ship looked like bathtub toys as they cruised miles away in the channel. Along the shore, the tide gurgled in and out, waves no bigger than a few inches. A gaggle of shore birds played tag with the bay, chasing the tide out, then turning and running across the sand as the tide chased them back in. A few seagulls squawked overhead. The day was sunny but cool, only in the high 60s, leaving the coastline devoid of sunbathers. A few jacketed walkers made their way along the shore. I crossed the sand and followed in their footsteps.

Walking along the sandy shores of the Chesapeake Bay didn't feel like exercise, something that was sorely lacking from my daily routine. But I could certainly use it. What is it about middle age that even though you eat less than you did as a youth, the pounds kept piling on? I wasn't overweight, per se, but my bikini days were far behind me. Heck, who was I fooling? I hadn't been in bikini-shape since the birth of my first son over thirty years ago.

It was almost two hours later when I hauled my tired self across the dunes to my little neighborhood of abandoned cottages. From this angle, the way the sun hit them, they looked charming. The neighborhood might be blighted (the exception being my pink cottage) but it had hope. I had hope.

A yellow taxi pulled up in front of Alva Rose's house. She climbed in the backseat. The cab pulled away from the curb and drove out of the neighborhood.

About the same time, a mail truck pulled down Waters Edge Lane. It zoomed up to Alva Rose's mailbox, delivered some mail, then zoomed back to the main road.

I looked up the street, then down, then back across the dunes. Not a single soul in sight. I was alone in the neighborhood.

Hmmm. There was mail in Alva Rose's mailbox. With, one supposed, her name. In bold-face type. If I took a peek, I could find out if that was, indeed, her real name. And perhaps more importantly, how she spelled her last name.

But tampering with U.S. Mail was a federal offense. And, I reminded myself, my goal was to stay out of jail.

Was it an offense to peek though? *No. It's a free world. I can look at anything,* I rationalized.

I debated the point while descending the dunes.

As I passed Alva Rose's driveway, the decision was made for me. My shoulder brushed the mailbox front and the lip dropped open. My gaze flitted—I mean lightening quick—and I saw the top piece of male was addressed to . . . Occupant. Damn!

What to do? What to do?

I reached my hand in and lifted the top letter ever so slightly, and peeked. Bingo. Addressed to Alva Rose. I couldn't quite make out the last name but it started with a big ell/little ell combination. So that part at least was correct.

I leaned in until my nose crossed the line and was inside the mailbox (it smelled like Krispy Kremes, for some reason) and as my eyes strained in the darkened space, I confirmed the spelling of Alva Rose's last name to be Llewellyn.

"What are you doing?"

I jumped at the voice. My head snapped around, my nose scraping on the edge of the rusty metal mailbox in the process. I turned to face Alva Rose as she climbed out of a cab which I hadn't even heard drive up.

"What are you doing?" Alva Rose repeated her question louder. And not in a friendly way.

"Oh, my goodness. You scared me!" I said.

Her body language was all *I'll thank you to not look in my mailbox, Miss Nosey Parker.*

Mine was all *Yes, I'm guilty of snooping through your mail.*

I took a deep breath, plastered a smile on my face, and did what any self-respecting middle-aged woman who'd been caught with her hand in the proverbial cookie jar would do . . . I lied. Like a rug.

"I'm trying to get my insurance changed over and I needed the zip code. I tried to wave down the mailman but he sped right past me. You weren't home when I knocked, so I thought I'd just peek at one of your letters. So, two-three-five-one-eight it is. I'm glad I checked because I had the last two numbers mixed up." *Shut up!* I told myself. The first rule of believable lies is *not* to babble like the town idiot.

No surprise, Alva Rose didn't seem to be buying my little white lie.

"I also wanted to invite you to dinner tonight," I said, all smiles and innocence. "I planned to throw some burgers on the grill and I hate to eat alone." I licked my dry lips. "I've got some questions about the area I'm hoping you can answer. And since it seems it's just you and me on this street, I thought we might be friends."

Hesitation on her part. I needed to sweeten the deal. Literally.

"I've got some cupcakes leftover for dessert."

That brought a twinkle to her aging eyes.

"Will six o'clock work for you?"

She nodded her acceptance.

"Six it is, then." I may have sounded a little *too* Gidget for such a casual invitation, but I countered that with a little Columbo indifference by dropping one shoulder, stepping back, and giving a quick salute. I turned and headed down the street towards my pink cottage, walking ever-so-casually, but the urge to run was *fierce*.

I heard Alva Rose tell the taxi driver, "Wait here while I grab my purse."

Just my luck that Alva Rose would forget her purse and come back and catch me with my nose in her mailbox. And now, somehow, I was beholden to whipping up dinner. My start on writing the next great American novel would have to wait another day.

As I scurried back home, I began thinking about what I needed to do in the next five hours in order to prepare dinner for two. Wait. What had I gotten myself into? Inviting a confessed killer to my house?

There had to be a logical explanation for Alva Rose's statement yesterday. Innocent until proven guilty, I reminded myself. Tonight, maybe after a few glasses of wine, I'd get to the truth and could let all the angst go.

I turned my thoughts towards compiling a mental shopping list of all the stuff I'd need to pull off the impromptu dinner party for two. First, I'd need the fixin's for another batch of triple-chocolate cupcakes, seeing as how I'd polished them off last night while Googling whether or not Alva Rose was a killer. Then I'd need food, a grill, and wine. Lots of wine. Three bottles, minimum.

Yes, three, for two people. Here's the way my wine-math works: First a bottle of a nice vintage to drink before Alva Rose arrives, in hopes of settling the butterflies in my stomach. The thought of being alone with a confessed killer made me a teensy bit nervous. Correction, a whole lotta nervous. The second bottle, of a slightly lesser vintage, would get us through dinner. Then a third, dare I say cheap (because let's be honest, after two bottles who's really gonna care what the last one tastes like?) dessert wine to share with Alva Rose while plying her with chocolate cupcakes and asking probing questions as to who exactly she'd killed, and why. Hey, that might make a great title for the novel I was about to write—Chilled Chardonnay and Chocolate Cupcakes Coerce Confessions.

On second thought, that might be a little too heavy on the alliteration.

I accomplished my shopping in less than an hour and had cupcakes baked and frosted by five p.m. That gave me time to shove the un-packed book boxes into the front room, set the card table in the dining alcove, and change into a plain white t-shirt that did not have chocolate-cake batter splattered on it, black shorts and Keds. Lastly, I put a flame to the charcoal briquettes. At quarter to six I opened my second bottle of wine, a La Crema Chardonnay.

After one last check in the mirror to ensure my clothes were clean and my hair in place, I headed back towards the kitchen. While walking through the front room, I heard someone talking on my front porch. I wasn't expecting anyone but Alva Rose.

Curious, but not wanting to be seen in case an unsavory character had wandered up onto my porch thinking the house was an easy score, I flattened myself against the wall near the front window. Ever so cautiously, I peeked over my shoulder to see who was out there. A tiny woman with blue-rinse curls and sporting an oversized hooded sweatshirt that had seen better days, leggings in a brown color that reminded me of doggie doo, and two-sizes-too-big orange Crocks. Guess I needn't have bothered getting cleaned up for dinner with Alva Rose.

She held a cell phone to her ear with one hand and gestured wildly with the other. I strained to hear what she was saying. Nothing but mumbled frustrations at first, but then she shouted loud enough for all of east Ocean View to hear, "If you do that, I'll kill you."

CHAPTER FIVE

I'll kill you . . . kill you . . .kill you.

We all make idle threats to kill, right? It's part of the generational lexicon. I'm guilty of it myself, having one time told Tasha, "If you tell my kids about this, I will kill you." The "this" had happened one moonlit night after way too many basil-lime martinis, when we'd decided it would be fun to go skinny dipping in her neighbor's pool. They'd traveled to Memphis, Tennessee, for a wedding. Or so we'd thought. About ten minutes into our frolic, the backyard lights blazed on and the owners came out to see what was going on. Most Humiliating Moment of My Life! And despite my threat, Tasha had blabbed to my boys the next day. Yet she remained alive and well. So yeah, we all make idle threats.

But still, with Alva Rose's track record . . .

I pulled out my phone and sent a quick text to Tasha: JUST HEARD ALVA ROSE SAY SHE WANTS TO KILL SOMEONE. FINGERS CROSSED IT'S NOT ME. SHE'S HERE FOR DINNER NOW. WILL SEND UPDATES AS SOON AS I KNOW SOMETHING. MISS YOU!

I hit SEND, and then slipped my phone back into my shorts' pocket. My heart skittered a bit as I cracked the door open and peeped through.

Alva Rose turned and looked at me.

"We'll talk later," she said into her cell phone then disconnected. She took a minute to settle the device into the pocket of her sweatshirt before looking in my direction. I wouldn't quite call her expression innocent, more like

25

sheepish.

I swung the door wide. "Is everything all right?" I asked.

"Oh, you heard that, huh?"

I nodded.

"Yeah, well . . ."

Silence descended between us. Of the awkward variety. We both seemed to be staring at her two-sizes-too-big Crocs.

"Damn Jane Ivy anyway!" she cried, her fists clenched and head tipped skyward. I felt a foot stomp coming on.

"Jane Ivy?" I asked tentatively.

"My baby sister."

More silence.

I had a hidden agenda for the evening, and it wouldn't be achieved standing in silence at my front door. Time to channel my inner Doris Day and make friends with the woman. "Sounds like you need a glass of wine as much as I do," I said.

Alva Rose nodded. She took a few steps towards my front door, and then bent down to retrieve a brown paper bag crumpled at the top like a Christmas popper. "Tomatoes, fresh from my garden. Thought they'd taste good on the burgers." She shoved the bag in my hands then stepped across the threshold.

As Alva Rose followed me to the kitchen, she said, "Love the upgrades. Huge improvement from when the last guy lived here. He decorated in early drug dealer. Gives hope for the rest of the houses."

"Are there plans to rehab the rest of the neighborhood?"

"If you've got an hour, I'll tell you all about the rise and fall of Waters Edge."

I had all evening. And I was curious about the area's evolution.

Alva Rose was a chatty one, once you got a little vino flowing through her veins. I heard all about how she'd moved to her house in 1958, back when The Skyrocket roller coaster was the big attraction a few blocks away at the Ocean View Amusement Park. "If the wind blew just right, you could smell the popcorn and hot dogs while sitting on my patio," she boasted. But times changed, beach goers made Virginia Beach their destination, and the area fell on hard times. Most of the homes on Waters Edge had been gobbled up by a real estate tycoon, but Alva Rose and her sister Janey Ivy had held out. Before the tycoon could tear down the properties and build a trendy seaside community of his dreams, the real estate market busted. Not long after that, the tycoon died and the heirs fought over the property while the houses stood empty and slipped into decay. One "young fella"—Alva Rose's term, and the way she said it meant he could be my age—finally made a deal on this little pink cottage, which had originally been a sickly green, and fixed it up. But he'd put more money into it than he could get out of it so decided to rent it until the rest of the street improved.

While Alva Rose had been talking, I'd been nibbling on salty cashews and sipping my oaky chardonnay. It was nice to have someone to talk to, or in this case, listen to. And if it weren't for that little issue of her murdering a man, I think Alva Rose and I could be great friends. Soon, very soon, I'd broach the subject.

Once the charcoal was ready, we grilled the burgers. I'd dressed the meat up with onion soup mix and sour cream and served them on toasted Kaiser Rolls with thick slices of red onions and even thicker slices of Alva Rose's fresh-from-the-garden tomatoes. I'd taken a few shortcuts with the sides, having not unpacked all my chef's tools yet. Stouffer's macaroni and cheese (with bread crumbs on top to give it the homemade look) served as a side dish. The veggie offering was a store-bought concoction of tomatoes, watermelon and basil sprinkled with a hint of sea salt. The quirky and seemingly discordant ingredients had tempted me. The results were nothing less than scrumptious.

Alva Rose continued her monologue of the personal

history of everyone who'd ever lived on Waters Edge. By the end of the meal I felt like I knew all of them, right down to their preference for flip-flops or Topsiders. What a hard-working—and hard-playing—bunch they'd been. In addition to the six or seven assembly plant workers and their families who had left the area after the Ford plant shut down in 2007, there was a collection of colorful characters who'd also called Waters Edge home, and whom Alva Rose considered family.

There was Nelly Sue Granger who had been a prostitute until she'd found Jesus. She now lived in a commune in Oklahoma. Poppy Simpson was a piano teacher, but had moved back to his hometown of Gary, Indiana to care for aging parents. He'd reunited with his childhood crush—his high school Spanish teacher by the name of Javier Ramos—and didn't expect to ever return to Waters Edge. Ginger Fieldstone had been known as the crazy cat lady, and after she'd been killed in a car accident, they'd had a heck of time rounding up over three dozen black cats and rehoming them. Frank Franklin had moved out after he'd made his first million as the Furniture Czar. (Even though I'd only been here two days, I'd heard enough of his annoying commercials to know there wasn't enough wine in the world to help me forget them!) Last to leave had been Trent Wiersteiner, aka T-Dub, when he'd disappeared from this very house ten years ago. "Nobody's seen hide nor hair of him since," she said.

Thus concluded the not-so-brief recount of Waters Edge residents.

I retrieved the cupcakes from the microwave where I'd stored them to keep the ants at bay, then carried them to the table. I sat and watched while Alva Rose ate three. I'd had my fill last night so instead chose to drink my dessert calories, a robust Chocovine chocolate raspberry wine. Don't knock it 'til you try it. De-lish!

Alva Rose's phone chirped. She fished it out of her pocket then glanced at the screen. "Damn it, Jane Ivy, I don't want to talk to you right now," she screamed at it while it continued to chirp. Eventually it fell silent and she placed it back in her pocket.

"Wanna talk about it?" I asked.

"No." She shifted in her seat then took a sip of wine before proceeding to talk about it. "My sister owns half of my house. She needs money to take her dream vacation to the Amalfi Coast, so says she's going to sell it. I can't afford to buy her out. But if I move, how will Rusty ever find me when he's ready to come home?"

Alva Rose took on the demeanor of a deflated balloon, as her whole body seemed to have lost its air. She withdrew into her seat and it looked as if her hooded sweatshirt was attempting to swallow her whole. A look of sadness spread down her face.

Now that I thought about it, I knew everything about everyone who had lived here for the last forty years, but she hadn't said a word about her own son. "Where's Rusty now?" I asked.

"Followed some young hussy back to her hometown in Idaho. I didn't approve of her and her druggy ways. Never should have made him choose between her and me." Alva Rose took a long sip of wine. She returned her goblet to the table and stared into the empty wine glass as if it might possibly hold all the answers to the universe. "I miss that boy of mine."

I took a deep breath. This was the opening I'd been waiting for. A chance to broach the subject. "You mentioned also that the day he left was the day you killed a man."

If I hadn't been studying her face, I would have missed the look of fear that passed across her features before settling into a forced half-smile. "I said that?"

"Yes, ma'am, you did."

"Huh. I must have been under the influence of chocolate or something. I haven't even thought about it for a long, long time."

"Do you wanna tell me about it?"

"Nothing to tell. Came home to find a man sleeping

on my couch. I grabbed a frying pan and bashed him in the head."

"So, it was self-defense?"

"He wasn't coming at me, if that's what you mean, but I was in fear for my life. All the neighbors had moved away so nobody would've heard me if I'd run outside and screamed for help. I didn't have a cell phone to call the cops. Way I figured it, it was kill or be killed."

I had my answer, but that only generated new questions. "Who was the guy?"

"If it's all the same to you, I'd rather not talk about it anymore."

I understood. There were things in my past I didn't want to talk about either, like walking into my husband's office and finding him canoodling with his secretary. Truth be told, they were more than canoodling—they were naked as jaybirds and having the time of their sexual lives. If I'd had a frying pan handy, I might have pulled an Alva Rose on the two of 'em. Hindsight being what it is, I wished I had.

We opened another bottle of chardonnay and talked into the wee hours of the next morning.

It wasn't until I was curled up under my soft pink blanket that I remembered I hadn't heard back from Tasha today. I hoped the twins were okay. I reached for my cell phone and sent her a quick voice-to-text assuring her all was well here.

CHAPTER SIX

*B*AM! BAM! BAM!

For the second morning in a row, the sound had me sitting up on the air mattress, blanket tucked under my chin, wondering what the hell was going on.

BAM! BAM! BAM!

Damn it! Tasha must have sent the police again.

A voice, muffled, came through the door. "Sydney Eleonore Tavaras, if you don't open this door right now, I'm gonna break it down!"

That was no Norfolk police officer. That was Tasha Kerns!

I was off the air mattress and half-crawled/half-ran to the door faster than you could say Best Friend Forever. My fingers fumbled turning the deadbolt, but eventually I got it open. I leapt onto the porch and wrapped Tasha in a big bear hug. I may have squealed a bit, which my mother would have said I was much too old to do, but what can I say? I was that happy to see a friendly face.

A cool breeze off the bay reminded me I was dressed only in a mid-drift teddy and bikini underwear, not suitable attire for any neighborhood, let alone one rife with people heading home after a night of partying. They might get the wrong impression of me. I jumped back across the threshold and pulled Tasha with me. We hugged again, accompanied by softer squeals, but squeals nonetheless. "What in the world are you doing here?" I asked.

"As soon as I got your text, I booked the next flight down. Six-fifty-five in the morning, thank you very much."

"What text?" I couldn't recall sending any message that would have Tasha on a plane at that ungodly hour. A morning person she was not.

"The one that Alva Rose wants to kill you."

"What?" I tried to think back to the texts I'd sent yesterday.

Tasha shoved her iPhone in my face. I read the text from me to her. HOPE TWINS ARE OK ALVA ROSE DOES WANT TO KILL ME.

Oops. "It's supposed to say 'doesn't.' As in does not."

"Are you sure you're okay?" She held me by the shoulders, her face awash with concern.

I nodded.

She pulled me close for another hug. "Thank gawd." She released me, but her hands held a tight clutch on my upper arms. She looked me right in the eyes. "Now I need coffee and details, in that order."

I laughed, but the sound gurgled in the back of my throat when I looked—truly looked—at my friend. I'd never seen her without full make-up and curly blond hair coiffed as if she'd just stepped out of a Rodeo Drive salon. Today she looked like she'd been to hell and back. All because of me. I had really scared her. Guilt was not a comfortable emotion for me. Time to make amends. "One mug of coffee coming right up." I turned in headed towards the kitchen.

We settled around the card table with steaming cups of instant brew. Between bites of turtle cupcakes (the best part of being an adult is having exactly what you want for breakfast), I explained to Tasha how Alva Rose had bashed an interloper in the head with a frying pan, and that she only said she wanted to kill Jane Ivy but didn't really mean it.

Tasha listened. Then she crooked her head to the side in a gesture I'd come to learn meant she was giving something serious thought. "I don't buy it."

Well, that surprised the hell out of me. "Why not?"

"You would have found something when you

Googled her. Something sensational about bashing in someone's head with a frying pan would have been all over the news. There would have been blood, I would think. And you know the old news adage, 'If it bleeds, it leads.' " She sat up taller in her seat. "There's more to this story, and I'm here to help you find out what."

"Huh?" I grabbed her coffee mug and took a big sniff. No odor of alcoholic spirits, yet this woman was talking like a crazy drunk. At 11:47 in the morning.

She grabbed her mug back and took a sip, grimaced, then put the mug back on the table before speaking. "I'll be Ernesta and you can be Gwendolyn."

"What are you talking about?"

"*The Snoop Sisters.*"

"Huh?"

"You know that old TV show starring Helen Hayes and Mildred Natwick?"

"Vaguely."

"We binge-watched all four episodes on your fifty-fifth birthday."

"We also drank Vodka Gimlets 'til the cows came home. I don't remember much."

"Let me refresh your memory, then. Ernesta Snoop and Gwendolyn Snoop Nickerson were two elderly sisters who wrote mysteries but solved a few murder cases along the way."

"Three counterpoints there." I ticked each one off on my fingers as I spoke. "One, we are not elderly. Two, we're not sisters, despite what you told the police. And three, we don't write mysteries."

"Okay. Good points. Bad analogy." She cocked her head to the side again. "Still—"

"And might I also bring up a fourth point. There's no need to solve a murder, as you put it, because we already know who the killer is."

"Alva Rose," we said in unison, although Tasha's exclamation was much more enthusiastic than mine.

"But," Tasha continued while flourishing a finger in

the air, "think of the fun we'll have finding the dead body."

"Honey, you and I obviously have different definitions of fun."

She laughed. "Maybe adventures would be a better word. Besides, the Wicked Witch of the North swooped down to spend time with her grandkids, so I have five days of freedom."

It's no secret that Tasha didn't get along with her step-mother-in-law, but to leave the woman in charge of the four rambunctious boys for five days bordered on diabolical.

"Who knows when I'll have time to myself again? It could be ten years or more. I want these days to be memorable." She sat back in her seat and gave me the Double-Dawg-Dare-You look that has gotten me into trouble on more than one occasion, to include that skinny-dipping incident. "So, are you in, Gwendolyn?" She wiggled her eyebrows and her mouth crooked ever so mischievously at the corner. And was that a twinkle in Tasha's tired eyes?

"I don't know—"

"Either you're with me or you're not, but I'm gonna solve this little mystery."

I gave a heavy sigh. If your best friend can't help you find a dead body, then who can? Heck, she is such a good friend I'd help her *move* a dead body. "What's the plan, then?"

"I don't have a plan yet. My brain is fuzzy due to lack of decent coffee. How far to the nearest Starbucks?" she asked while pushing her mug of instant sludge away from her.

"About five blocks." I once again took in her disheveled appearance and knew, as her BFF, I couldn't let her start her search for a dead body looking like a Raggedy Anne doll some puppies had fought over. "How 'bout I make a coffee run while you jump in a shower?"

She agreed and headed upstairs to shower and make herself presentable.

I got in my car and headed east. While driving, I attempted to noodle up a strategy to get Tasha back on a plane to Cleveland and me out of the dead-body-finding business. Apparently, I was suffering from caffeine deficiency myself, as not a single scheme came to mind. Maybe because my subconscious wanted my friend to stay with me for as long as she could, no matter the week's entertainment.

Once back at my little pink cottage by the sea, I parked the car, and then grabbed the Starbucks Traveler off the floor of my truck. What two people were going to do with three-quarters of a gallon of high-octane coffee didn't bear thinking about. We wouldn't be napping the day away, that's for sure. "Tasha," I called, as I entered the house. No answer. I put the disposable coffee jug on the table and went looking for her. I searched the entire house. No Tasha to be found.

I raced to the front porch and scanned the street. Had some desperate drug attic waltzed in and carried my BFF away?

Before I could get too worked up at that worse-case scenario, I looked over towards Alva Rose's house and saw my neighbor and Tasha hunkered down in old, low-slung beach chairs and chatting up a storm.

Let the games begin.

CHAPTER SEVEN

Alva Rose will be here any minute and yet you're still wearing your bathing suit," Tasha said to me. The two women had bonded during their chat this morning and had decided we all should take shag-dancing lessons this evening. Come to find out, Tasha had *always* wanted to learn. Geez, you think you know a woman and then you find out something like that.

The last thing I wanted to do was go drinking and dancing. It had been an exhausting day of shopping in an effort to make progress on the fun—but daunting—task of furnishing my coastal cottage. Now I was nestled in the thick ropes of my new Outer Banks Hammock, the only piece of "furniture" we'd purchased thus far. Well, that and another air mattress for Tasha to sleep on. It's not like I'd let my best friend sleep on a cold hardwood floor. Such lack of hospitality would have my mother turning in her grave.

"You don't have to go if you don't want to," Tasha said.

I put my arm up to shade the sun from my eyes and saw my friend standing there in Beach Chic attire. I don't know how she has the perfect outfit for every occasion. It's her special power.

"What makes you think I don't want to?" I asked.

"Because you don't seem to be making an effort to get dressed."

"You go on without me." I closed my eyes and wished Tasha away.

"But I need your help." I felt the hammock sag where Tasha sat down. I rolled to counterbalance the weight shift. "Listen to the plan I came up with to get Alva Rose to confess about who she killed."

I cracked one eye open and looked at her.

"We'll get her totally schnockered and she'll confess. Brilliant, no?"

I'd read a few Nancy Drew books in my youth, yet I didn't recall the girl detective using that particular method of getting a suspect to talk. But then, Tasha was no Nancy Drew.

"Plus, we'll have some fun dancing in the process. Win-win."

The doorbell rang,

"That'll be Alva Rose ready to party the night away. We're leaving in fifteen minutes, with or without you, so hurry."

I didn't exactly hurry, but did manage to get changed into a soft pink golf shirt, slim-cut ankle-length white capris and strappy leather sandals before our Uber ride arrived.

The parking lot of Betty's Beach Bar by the Bay was half-empty, but the party was in full swing. "Build Me Up Buttercup" blared from the outdoor speakers and we sang along as we shimmied and strolled our way through the crowd to the bar, the décor of which was quintessential crab-shack. Tasha ordered a round of Lancaster Lemonades, which is a tasty concoction of vodka, Limoncello and a splash of Ginger Ale. OPERATION: GET ALVA ROSE SOZZLED was in full swing.

The crowd was eclectic, everything from conservatively dressed retired folks down to those barely of legal drinking age and not wearing much in the way of clothing. We drank lovely Lancaster Lemonades. We shag danced under the careful instruction of Miss Mel. We talked (more like yelled) and laughed at the shaggers who acted like they were in the final rounds of *Dancing with the Stars,* if only in their minds. Adding to the evening was the fantastic beach-vibe and music that took me back to my high school days with songs like "Under the Boardwalk" and "Shama Lama Ding Dong." It was the most fun I'd had in years. Maybe in my life, thanks to the great company, and many, many rounds of lovely libations.

The evening was winding down and Alva Rose was having trouble remaining seated on the bench seat between Tasha and me. She kept slipping lower and lower until only her mop of blue-rinse curls peeped above the table. Laughing hysterically, Tasha and I grabbed Alva Rose by the armpits and tugged her up into a sitting position. She hadn't spoken a coherent word since the last round of drinks, and I had written off our plan to get any information out of her this evening. Lesson learned: don't expect Alva Rose to keep up the drinking pace of Tasha and me. We were, after all, practically professionals.

Imagine my surprise when she pointed to a blonde pony-tailed woman in skimpy clothes walking by our table. Alva Rose said, as clear as you please, "That's the sister of the man I killed." With that, Alva Rose's eyes rolled up in her head and she slipped quietly and unceremoniously under the table.

Tasha and I looked at each other, then down at Alva Rose.

"Let's go talk to the sister," Tasha said while pushing me off the bench seat ahead of her.

"We can't leave Alva Rose on the floor like that."

Tasha sighed. "You're right."

We struggled and got Alva Rose stretched out on the bench as fast as we could.

The dead man's sister was heading for the exit at a pretty good clip, given the four-inch heels she was wearing.

By the time we got out the door, all we saw were the taillights of the taxi turning west on Shore Drive.

"Dang," I said. "So much for that lead. And I doubt we'll get any more out of Alva Rose tonight."

"Don't give up so easily." Tasha grabbed me by the arm and frog-marched me in the direction of the bar.

"There's a whole line of men who noticed those long legs and jiggly ass. All we have to do is cozy up to them and find out what her name is."

Again, not in the Nancy Drew School of Sleuthing Manual. And my cozying-up-to-strange-men skills were rusty after thirty-two years of marriage. Not that they had ever been all that great to begin with.

I stood back while Tasha wiggled her way between two aging surfer types. In less than thirty seconds she turned around and flashed me a winning smile. "Our work here is done," she said. "Time to head home and start our cyber search."

We collected our belongings, to include Alva Rose, and headed for the door. It was a struggle to escort our stumbling, mumbling friend, but we did.

"That was easier than I thought," Tasha said as we waited for the Uber. "Her last name is Smith."

"What's so easy about the name Smith? First, it sounds made-up, and second, there must be thousands of Smiths in the area."

"Don't worry, her first name is something unusual. Brooke, I think."

"You think?"

"I'm pretty sure."

I pulled out my cell phone and Googled the name. "There are thirteen Brooke Smiths listed in the area. Between the white pages and ancestry-dot-com, we'll know everything we need to know before the night is through." This part of sleuthing I was good at.

"Smith is her married name," Tasha added.

"You didn't happen to get her maiden name, did you?"

"I did. Sort of. My source, Gary, mumbled a convoluted name that I hope I'll remember when I hear it."

It was an uneventful ride home and we quickly got Alva Rose settled on her old orange sofa, and then raced back to my house. Armed with a can of Pringles potato chips for sustenance (and to counteract the effect of the Lancaster Lemonades) and chilled bottles of Aquafina (also to counter-act the effect of the Lancaster Lemonades), we set down in front of my iPad to find out what we could about Brooke Smith.

It was shortly after two a.m. when we finally got down to the root of it all.

Tasha sat cross-legged on the floor, huddled up with my iPad while I stretched out on the inflatable mattress next to her, snuggled up in my pink blanket. "Got it," she cried. "Brooke's maiden name is Wiersteiner."

"What?" That brought me to a sitting position.

"Wiersteiner." She spelled it out. "I told you it was an unusual name. I'd never heard it before."

"I have," I said. "Someone by that name used to live in this house. First name Trent." I'd remembered that because my first boyfriend in third grade had the same name. He'd moved to Milwaukee over the ensuing summer and that was the end of that relationship. I hadn't given him a second thought until I'd heard his name yesterday, and not again until now.

"What are the odds of it being the same guy?" Tasha asked, her fingers clicking rapidly over the tablet's keyboard. "Apparently pretty good."

"Alva Rose told me he was a drug dealer."

"No mention of that here. But it does say he disappeared ten years ago, and nobody has heard from him since."

It took me a few moments to put words to what I'd figured out. Goose pimples danced up my arms, and hairs on the back of my neck jumped up to full-attention stance. "Nobody has seen him since because Alva Rose killed him."

"Well then," Tasha said, cocking her head to one side. "I wonder where she hid the body."

CHAPTER EIGHT

Let's stage an intervention," Tasha said the next morning over coffee.

We were both still wearing our clothes from last night as we sat across from each other at my card table. The metal chairs felt particularly cold and hard. And while the plantation shutters were shut against the light, I could feel sunshine and sand beyond. My eyes ached. My body ached. My soul ached. Yeah, it was that bad.

"What do you mean by an 'intervention'? Alva Rose isn't a heroin addict or anything." I thought about how little I knew about my new neighbor. "At least I don't think she is. Maybe a choc-o-holic."

"Not a drug intervention. An information intervention, where we get her to spill the beans about Trent."

"Really?" I looked over the rim of my mug. We'd reheated the Starbucks from yesterday. There wasn't much there, but it would get us started. I took a sip and tried not to grimace at the bitterness unique to day-old coffee. "You really want to pursue this?"

"You betcha. To its logical conclusion. If you kill someone in self-defense, the body doesn't just disappear. I want to find out why Alva Rose panicked and what she did with the body. Maybe she tossed it into the bay and it floated out to sea and became some great white's dinner."

"Enough," I said, raising my hand. "Not on my queasy stomach."

"You used to be able to hold your liquor better than

that. You must be getting old."

"No need to remind me." As much as I hated to admit it, I did feel old this morning. Old and hungover. Not a good combination.

Tasha reached across and patted my hand resting on the table. "I'm kidding. You're in the prime of life. And the dead body in the bay, that's only one theory. Bottom line, Trent Wiersteiner's body has never been found. My gut tells me there's still more to this story. Don't tell me for a second your gut isn't screaming the same thing."

"The only thing my gut tells me is to turn it over to the police."

"Where's the fun in that?"

"Again, you and I have a different definition of that word."

"I gotta tell you, Syd, I'm loving this." Tasha's eyes literally sparkled. "Getting those guys to talk about Brooke last night? What a kick. Even got an adrenaline rush searching the Internet for clues, knowing that each click could bring us closer to an answer. I know there's more excitement ahead. I can feel it. Maybe I'll become a PI when I get back to Cleveland."

"You? A PI?" I snorted. My mother would have said that it's not appropriate for a woman my age—or any age, for that matter—to snort, but it pretty much summed up how I felt about Tasha's new career choice.

"I'll get Chad to come in the business with me," she said.

"Yeah, like Chad will give up his well-paying corporate accounting job in order to help you spy on cheating husbands."

"We'd be like Nick and Nora Charles from *The Thin Man* movies."

Gawd, I loved William Powell and Myrna Loy. They were the perfect on-screen couple. "Tasha, I'm your best friend, so I feel I should be the one to tell you that you and your hubby are no Nick and Nora."

"Ha ha ha. Maybe not the nineteen-thirties version,

but I think we could reinvent them for the twenty-first century."

"That'll be between you and Chad. Right now, it's you and me, though. And while I'm not up for an intervention, as you call it, I do think we should go check on Alva Rose. Maybe take her some coffee. She's gonna have one hell of a headache." I knew that because if hers was half as bad as mine, she'd be willing to swear off chocolate for the rest of her life in order to silence the jackhammers thumping away inside her skull.

A slow, devilish smile spread across Tasha's face. "You gave me a great idea." She jumped up from the table, grabbed yesterday's Starbuck's Traveler from the fridge and headed towards the front door. "Come on," she said.

I looked down at my empty mug with no recollection of consuming the contents. It hadn't even begun to take the edge off the hangover. I needed more coffee, lots more coffee, and the supply had headed out the door. I got up slowly and followed at a pace that didn't make my head hurt too much. All this for coffee. But also to check on a friend, I reminded myself.

If I were to be one-hundred percent honest with myself, though, a little part of me needed to hear how Alva Rose had disposed of Trent Wiersteiner's body. I had complete faith that Tash would wheedle it out of her one way or the other.

But I had no idea Tasha could be so diabolical.

I entered Alva Rose's kitchen—which was every bit as drab and dated as her living room—to find Tasha waving a plate of what looked like week-old corned beef hash under my elderly neighbor's nose. If the old dear was even one-tenth as queasy as I was after a night of Lancaster Lemonades, then that would qualify as torture under the Geneva Convention. One look at the pale pink meat and chunks of gray-ish potatoes and I practically tossed my cookies, and I was all the way across the room.

Alva Rose's face was positively green.

"Tell us where you buried Trent's body and I'll swap

out the hash with Saltine crackers," Tasha promised.

Alva Rose's head snapped up at the mention of Trent's name. "How did you know . . ."

"A detective never reveals her sources," Tasha said. "Suffice it to say we know you killed him. Wanna tell us what happened?" She waved the plate of hash under Alva Rose's nose.

Alva Rose leaned as far back in her chair as she could to get away from the revolting food. "Crackers first, then I'll talk," she said in the raspiest voice I'd ever heard. It kind of scared me. If a body could speak from the grave, I imagined it would sound like that. I shuddered off the creepy feeling making its way up my spine.

Tasha nodded towards an old Saltine tin, the likes of which I hadn't seen since my grandmother's pantry, sitting on the ragged Formica counter near me. Fortunately, the crackers inside were of this century. Once I had the clip off and the waxed paper open, I tried one, and they were sufficiently crunchy to pass as step one in the morning's hangover cure. I laid the package on the table, then backed away to my corner where I could watch the proceedings.

Alva Rose selected a cracker and chewed slowly. Very, very slowly. At one point I thought she'd fallen asleep while chewing, but then her mouth moved again. Eventually, she swallowed.

She reached for another cracker, but Tasha pulled them out of her reach.

Alva Rose sighed, wiped the crumbs off the table, folded her hands, rested them on the table, and then began to tell us the story.

"Manda Haskins. She's the daughter I never had. She and Rusty dated all through high school. Them two were prom king and queen." Alva Rose paused.

Tasha pushed the sleeve of crackers closer. Alva Rose took one but didn't eat it. Instead she held the corners between her pointer fingers and spun it around and around. Tasha and I exchanged glances, but neither one of us spoke.

Alva Rose resumed her story, her voice quivering as if on the verge of tears. "Everyone knew they'd get married. But Manda was some kinda smart. She got a full scholarship and went off to UVA and married some hotshot lawyer and they settled up in DC. Rusty never married anyone else. When Manda's momma took ill, she moved back home. Manda and her husband were divorced by then. Never did have any kids. I really hoped she and Rusty would get back together." Elva Rose pulled a long, drawn-out sigh. "They hung out together a few times, but by now Rusty was with Lina. Her real name was Carolina Blue, but everyone called her Lina. I called her trouble."

Alva Rose popped the Saltine in her mouth and chewed. Slowly. I was getting impatient and wished Alva Rose would tell us what we wanted to know and be done with it.

Tasha sat slouched in her chair as if she had all the time in the world.

Eventually Alva Rose stopped chewing and spoke. "These crackers sure are dry. There's a co-cola in the fridge there, if you wouldn't mind getting it for me. I don't have the energy right now . . ."

Tasha nodded once, but didn't move towards the fridge. That left it to me to grab the cold beverage, wondering what kind of person preferred pop over coffee in the morning. Must be a beach-life thing.

I found the fridge stocked with generic cola, selected a can, popped the top then slid it across the table to Alva Rose.

She took a long, long swig. Then silence, broken by a long, long belch.

No apology, just silence.

Patience is not my virtue, and I couldn't stand the suspense of Alva Rose's delay. I cleared my throat. Both Alva Rose and Tasha looked at me.

"You were telling us about the Rusty/Manda/Lina love triangle," I prompted.

Alva Rose nodded. "I was hoping that Rusty and

Manda would get back together, but then that snake in the grass T-Dub—that's short for T-Double U—the guy you call Trent Wiersteiner, started nosing in. I saw him with Manda a few times down at Betty's, and they looked much too cozy for my liking. I decided to have a chat with the boy. He rented that house you're in now." She looked at me.

I nodded. We'd already figured that out, brilliant detectives that we were.

"Anyway, he'd been a big help to me when I had back issues. Fixed me up with some, ah, let's say a little somethin'-somethin', to help take the edge off my pain. I called him and asked him for a refill, thinking when he delivered, I would warn him away from Manda.

"I came home one night and found him asleep on my sofa. I don't know how he got in, as I always keep my doors and windows locked in this neighborhood. You'd be wise to do the same," she said to me.

I nodded. Again, something I already knew.

"I'd come from playing Bunco with my old-lady friends. We don't so much play as we do gossip, and the story had come up about T-Dub and Manda. And then more stories about T-Dub and Lina. That boy was fixin' to break my son's heart, from every angle. And you know how us mommas are. So, when I came in and saw him sleeping on the sofa, I had worked up a powerful rage. I wanted to have a talk with that boy, and he lay there sleeping like an innocent babe. I shook him but he didn't wake up." Alva Rose's voice rose a few decibels and I could feel the anger she had now in a ten-year-old memory. I can only imagine what kind of rage she'd been in that night.

"I shouted. And the more he slept and denied me speaking my piece, the angrier I got. And I don't know what got into me. I looked around for something that would get his attention, and when I went into the kitchen to get something to drink, I saw my iron skillet there on the stove."

I glanced towards the old stove. A heavy cast iron

skillet sat on the back burner. I had fond memories of one just like that my grandma used to make the best cornbread. It lost its innocence now that I knew it was a weapon of murder.

"I picked it up," Alva Rose said, "and felt its weight and knew that would get his attention. I marched right back out there and smacked that boy right over the head. But he still didn't wake up. That got me a bit worried. He must be under the influence of some powerful drugs himself, although he had a history of staying away from drugs and drinks. I checked for a pulse, and that's when I realized he was dead. I'd killed him. I didn't think I'd hit him that hard, but there was anger in my swing."

Tears started trickling down her cheeks, then her shoulders began shaking. "I think I'm gonna be sick," she cried as she got up from the table and staggered down the hall to what I could only presume was the bathroom.

We heard the dulcet tones of someone tossing their cookies. Or in Alva Rose's case, her Saltine crackers.

"I'm outta here," Tasha said. She's a great mom, but had never been one to handle the sound of retching. She runs out of movies at the first sign of gratuitous vomiting, which seems to be all the rage any more. Another reason we both preferred classic movies.

I hung around and helped Alva Rose settle on the sofa, crackers and co-cola in arms reach before following Tasha back to my little pink cottage. We'd gotten what we'd come for, confirmation that Alva Rose had killed Trent Wiersteiner, aka T-Dub.

Mystery solved. But there was no happiness in knowing the truth.

My heart went out to the dear old lady. I know that orange is the new black, but it wouldn't be a good color on Alva Rose. Not at all.

CHAPTER NINE

Tash," I called as I entered my new home, but my greeting was met with silence. "Tash," I called again. Still no answer. "Natasha Olivia Bernsdorf Kerns," I hollered, my voice tinged with an undercurrent of impatience. It wasn't like Tasha not to answer and I wanted to talk through my intentions to report what we know to the police.

My sandy feet scratched against the hardwood floors as I went from room to room. The 4Runner was still in the driveway so she hadn't driven off for fresh coffee. What could have happened to her in the last twenty minutes? My imagination ramped up from perfectly safe to lying in a pool of blood in 3.2 seconds. That's a talent of mine, to think the most horrific thing possible had happened. She could have slipped on a wet tile floor and knocked her head on the sink and was now bleeding out, or she could have caught some drug-crazed thief rummaging through my meager belongings and tried to stop him, and he'd shot her through the gut. My worst-case scenarios can run the full danger spectrum, from innocent to diabolical.

I tried to tamp down the gurgle of fear as I increased the pace of my search, which eventually led me to the backyard. I found Tasha stretched out in the hammock, her right arm crooked across her eyes to shield the late-morning sun. No blood. Breathing peacefully. Sleeping the sleep of one who had partied too hard the night before. Once again, I'd worried for naught. You'd think I'd have learned that after all these years of worry and self-inflicted anxiety.

"Tash," I called again, but her only answer was a soft, raspy snore.

Should I wake her? No, she'd only talk me out of what I wanted to do, since she had her heart set on finding where the body was buried. I had no explanation for this detective streak she'd developed since coming to visit, but one thing I love about Tasha is if she says she's going to do something, she does it. I have complete faith she will solve this backwards murder investigation. But at what cost? Alva Rose in jail?

While in my heart I felt sympathy for Alva Rose, in my head I knew I needed to report the murder to the police. It was the right thing to do. Alva Rose had had ten years to turn herself in, and I doubted there was anything I could say now to change her mind.

I'd report the murder, then find her the best attorney the free legal-aid society could provide.

The phone call to Officer Grant was anti-climactic. He didn't sound at all interested but said he'd stop by and have a chat with her. I guess there wasn't much urgency, as Alva Rose didn't seem like much of a flight risk (she was probably sleeping the sleep of an over-indulger, too), and it's been a decade. Was one more day of T-Dub in the ground going to compromise any evidence? Doubtful.

Somehow, I thought being a responsible citizen would have felt better. Instead, it seemed as if a 10-ton weight had crawled up my back and settled on my shoulders. While I'd only known Alva Rose for a short time, I thought of her as my friend. Maybe it was the Lancaster-Lemonade bonding experience, or it could be a two-lonely-people-living-on-a-lonely-street connection. But I considered us friends, and friends don't report friends to the police.

While I unpacked a few boxes of kitchen items, I tried to picture Alva Rose raising a heavy cast iron skillet high in the air and slamming it down on a sleeping man's head, crushing his skull and sending him to his final reward. But the mental image wouldn't come together, no matter how hard I tried. She didn't have the heart of a killer. Or the strength in those scrawny arms to do fatal damage. Plus, she'd seemed so remorseful telling us her story. It wasn't like a premeditated thing, but murder is still murder, no matter how you look at it.

Thoughts of Alva Rose as a killer somehow sloshed around in my head until they turned into thoughts of Rusty as a killer. Alva Rose hadn't heard from him in over a decade, since the day T-Dub was killed. Kind of suspicious, if you ask me.

Had he had a role in this?

Could Alva Rose have told us a story to protect her only son? He'd certainly have had a motive in jealousy of T-Dub moving in on his women, plural. But motive enough to kill? A punch in the nose, for sure, but killing? Not knowing the first thing about Rusty other than his name and his affection for fudge, I couldn't say. But maybe it made a tiny bit of sense.

It seemed to me the missing piece to the puzzle at this point was Rusty.

I looked out the window where Tasha slept. I didn't have the heart to wake her just to share my wild imaginings. I needed some facts.

Time for another on-line search. I reached for my phone and got to Googling.

Seems you can find anyone anywhere in the world. I'd never appreciated the online white pages before. Sure makes life simple. As a child, you needed a city and state for the operator to find a number for you. I only had a general area of the country, but with a few keystrokes, I found an R. Llewellyn in Murtaugh, Idaho.

I called the number and left a simple message on his home phone. "Your momma needs you." It's not like I could say, "Your momma confessed to killing T-Dub. You need to man-up and get back here and face the music." That could have had him skipping the country. I hoped he loved his momma enough to call and find out the latest, and not let her take the rap.

I couldn't think of anything else to do to help Alva

Rose at the moment.

As I finished breaking down the last packing box, Tasha stumbled into the kitchen. "Coffee," she mumbled and slumped into the metal chair across from me.

And coffee she got, of the dreaded instant variety.

"Listen," I said as I slid a steamy cup of strong coffee under her nose. "I've been thinking."

"Hold that thought," she said as she drank the nectar of the gods in a few big gulps. "Okay, I'm ready."

I laid out my thoughts on Rusty's involvement, explained my phone call to his home, and then confessed that I wished I hadn't been so quick to report Alva Rose's confession to Officer Grant.

A movement outside my front window caught my eye. I looked out to see a police car cruising down Waters Edge towards the main road.

I recognized Alva Rose's curly hair profiled in the back seat.

"Oh, no! They've got her." Officer Grant hadn't waited too long to confront her. He must have believed me.

I needed to redact my accusation and make sure Alva Rose didn't spend a minute behind bars on account of me. I jumped out of my seat, grabbed my purse and keys and headed for the door. "Come on. We've got to spring her."

* * * * * *

The "springing" of a confessed murderer is not as easy as one would think. There was nothing Tasha and I could do or say to convince Officer Grant my earlier reports could very well be erroneous. He said all reports of crime—especially murder—are taken seriously by the Norfolk Police Department, and all are fully investigated.

So, we sat in the dreary waiting room of the police station, which was depressing as hell. Officer Grant and some detective whose name I didn't catch and didn't like on sight—he was, in a word, squirrely—grilled Alva Rose.

They had the right to hold her for twenty-four hours.

At four o'clock we gave up and Tasha and I headed over to Betty's Beach Bar to drown our frustrations. My heart was heavy. So much guilt and helplessness. I wish I'd never made that phone call.

We snagged two stools at the counter and settled in to nurse our first round of Lancaster Lemonades of the day.

Even though it was late afternoon on a sunny fall day, the interior of the beach bar was dim. And crowded. We soon learned there was a dance contest getting ready to start, so lots of shaggers were warming up, movin' and grovin' to "Heard it Through the Grapevine."

I watched the dancers with interest, but all I could think about was Alva Rose in the backseat of the police cruiser.

"I feel awful," I said to Tasha. "The thought of Alva Rose in a cold, dank holding cell with all manner of drunks and drug addicts and prostitutes as her cellmates. It breaks my heart." I shuddered against the image.

"Me, too." Tasha patted my arm.

The woman seated next to us leaned over and said, "I didn't mean to listen in on your conversation, but you aren't talking about Alva Rose Llewellyn who lives out on Waters Edge, are you?"

We nodded.

"She's in jail? What for, squishing a bug?" The woman laughed. "Why, that woman doesn't have a mean bone in her tiny body."

"She confessed to killing Trent Wiersteiner," Tasha told her.

"No shit? Hey Toby," she called over to the bartender. "Alva Rose is in jail. Can you believe it?"

"What for," he asked.

"She killed T-Dub."

"What?" a woman with a dolphin tattoo on her shoulder yelled, "Hey, Sammy Boy, come here. You gotta hear this."

It snowballed from there. We'd tell one person, then

that person would call another bar patron over with, "Hey, you gotta hear this."

I let Tasha enjoy her fifteen minutes of fame while I sipped my tangy drink and watched the group on the dance floor. Dancers danced to "Under the Boardwalk" and I hummed quietly along. That was another song that brought back memories of my youth, both happy and sad.

One of the contestants caught my attention. She was tall, lithe, and had long, untamed, sandy-blond hair that swung below her shoulders. But what had held me mesmerized was the way she danced with smooth and sexy moves. How she managed it all in four-inch high heels defied logic. Something about the girl seemed familiar, but since I didn't know a soul in southeastern Virginia it must be a case of her reminding me of someone back in Ohio.

When the conversation around me reduced to whispers, I turned to find out what secrets were being told.

"I'm sure as hell not gonna tell her."

"Chicken."

"You tell her, big man."

"Oh, for gawd's sake, I'll do it," said the woman with the dolphin tattoo. "Gimme a shot of tequila first, though."

I leaned into Tasha. "What are they talking about?"

"Who's gonna break the news to T-Dub's sister, Brooke."

Brooke was here? I looked around the crowded room. The music swelled. The audience clapped for the dancers as they meandered back towards their tables.

The bearer of bad news slipped off her barstool and made her way across the room. She slipped into a chair next to the high-heel wearing blonde who had captured my attention. She leaned in and spoke into the other woman's ear.

Aha, that's why the woman had looked familiar. We'd seen her last night walking out of the bar. Brooke Wiersteiner Smith.

A few minutes later Brooke got up and headed down the hall towards the Little Gulls Room (as opposed to the

Little Buoys room. Beach bars, gotta love 'em.)

Blame the crazy impulse on the Lancaster Lemonades, which gave me the idea—and the courage—to follow her. My reason wasn't really clear, but my compulsion was not to be ignored.

When I got there, Brooke was already in the stall. I could hear her talking. A quick peak under the stall confirmed the high-heel-wearing woman and I were alone. She was talking. To someone on a cell phone? While she did her business. *Eewwww.* I blocked out the splashing noise and focused on the conversation.

"Can you believe Alva Rose confessed to killing T-Dub?" She chuckled a bit, then paused. "I know. Can't imagine why. Do you think she suspects the truth? I mean, seriously, after all these years." Another pause.

I used the downtime to process the information. Brooke had indicated someone other than Alva Rose killed T-Dub. It could be anyone, I suppose. *Hmmmm.* Would Alva Rose take the fall for anyone other than her son?

Brooke flushed, muffling her side of the conversation.

Panic set in when I realized she'd be coming out of the stall any moment. I did *not* want her to find me. I wasn't prepared to interrogate a witness. Those sorts of things were best left to the professionals, or at least Tasha. Fight or flight? Hands down, *flight!* I turned and reached for the door, giving it a good hard tug. It slipped from my sweating hand and slammed shut with a loud *bang* that echoed in the cold, cavernous restroom.

The door to the stall opened.

We locked gazes, Brooke and me. Her eyes narrowed until they were little, tiny, accusing slits. "How long you been standing there?" she growled.

"Just walked in," I answered, with Sandra Dee spunk and innocence.

"Did you see anyone else?"

Don't ask me why but it seemed like a good idea to lie. It wasn't a conscious decision. The words rolled out of my mouth. "Yeah, some girl in a white denim skirt just rushed out. She looked to be in a big hurry to get back to join her friends." I'm not sure why I'd thrown some random woman under the bus, but I hoped she'd forgive me. She hadn't been one of the shag dancers, but she'd made an impression on me when she'd walked in and slid into a booth with some other beach-bar people.

Brooke studied me through narrowed eyes. It made my skin crawl and my heart beat erratically. I don't think she believed me, so I'd have to convince her otherwise.

I waggled my fingers in the air, in the universal motion of needing to wash off stickiness. "Spilled my drink. I know, a waste of good alcohol, but what can I say?" I sashayed past Brooke to the sink and turned on the water.

"A white skirt, you say?" she asked.

I nodded.

"Damn it," Brooke said. "If she overheard, then I'm a dead woman."

CHAPTER TEN

No sooner had I settled onto my barstool than my cell phone buzzed. It was Alva Rose calling to see if we would give her a ride home from the local lockup. She was being released, on account of the police didn't have a case if they didn't have a body. All they had was my word (that she'd admitted to me to whacking T-Dub over the head with an iron skillet) against her word (that she hadn't killed anyone). And if she hadn't killed anyone, how could she know where the body was?

Hard to argue that.

Tasha drove, since she hadn't managed more than a sip of her drink on account of she'd been so busy telling Alva Rose's murder-confession story to anyone who would listen. There'd been plenty who'd wanted to listen. This was a small, tight, beach community where everyone had their nose in everyone else's business.

On the way, I told Tasha about my Little Gulls Room encounter with Brooke.

"So, what do you deduce?" sleuth Tasha asked.

"I'm more convinced than ever that Alva Rose is covering for Rusty," I responded. "But I'm thinking Brooke knows what happened, too, and for some reason she's covering for Rusty as well. But what's her connection to the woman wearing a white skirt? And why would she say, 'I'm a dead woman?' I gotta be honest, that kind of spooked me. But certainly, she meant that in the figurative, not the literal, sense." I paused to formulate additional deductions. "The person Brooke was talking to on the phone knows, too. That might be a key piece of the puzzle, but how in the world are we ever going to find out who that was?" I stared out of the window at the mish-mash of splendor and near-squalor that defined this bayside community. "It makes me wonder what the Brooke-Rusty connection is."

We drove the last few miles in silence. I used the time to examine the facts from every angle possible but couldn't come up with any other explanation for Alva Rose's false confession, unless she was covering for someone. Rusty, of course, seemed the obvious choice to me, but it's been my experience—my movie-watching experience, that is— not to zone in on one theory until all of the evidence is in. *Witness for the Prosecution*, starring Tyrone Power and Marlene Dietrich, taught me that.

Wait, here's a thought. Alva Rose also seemed to have regard for Rusty's high-school girlfriend Manda. Alva Rose seemed to be holding on to the fantasy that someday Manda and Rusty would get married and live happily ever after. And if Manda killed T-Dub, and Rusty had deep feelings for her, he might have helped kill, or at least get rid of the body for her. Yes, I could imagine a frantic phone call to the first love of her life. "I need help." And in he'd rush. Then skedaddle out of town to avoid prison for his role.

But then where do Brooke, the woman in the white skirt, and the person on the other end of the phone come into the picture?

We found Alva Rose sitting on a wooden bench in the waiting room. She stood when she saw us and scurried, head down, out of the station. We followed her to my trusty 4Runner, then we all piled in, buckled up, and headed for home.

Alva Rose seemed disinclined to talk. Can't say as how I blamed her. In old movies they depict interrogation rooms as small, dismal cement-block spaces with a metal table and a miserable looking metal chair or two. Then there was the *de rigueur* single lightbulb dangling overhead, and a detective pacing around the table, lobbing louder and more incriminating questions until the suspect cracked and copped to the crime. I pictured Alva Rose hunkered down in a chair, her curls barely visible above the table top, and the lone bulb casting dark shadows across her craggy face. Hours and hours of questioning, no food nor water, just the detective lobbing accusations until something stuck. My heart about broke at the image.

How exactly does one apologize for putting another in that position? I doubted even Hallmark could come up with the proper sentiments. But I did owe Alva Rose something.

I turned to her in the backseat. She sat huddled in the corner staring out the window. "I'm so sorry," I said.

"Who's hungry?" Tasha asked.

The truck took a sharp turn and I had to grab onto the O-Shit! handle above the window to keep myself in my seat. I looked around to see we were pulling into a parking spot at Del's Diner.

Tasha said, "I read on *Yelp!* they've got a great crab burger here."

"What are you talking about?" I asked. "We were gonna—"

Tasha shot me a look that hushed me up. She lifted her eyes towards the front door of the establishment where a long-legged woman in a short, white, denim skirt was heading inside. It was the woman we'd seen at Betty's not more than an hour ago. The one Brooke seemed worried had overheard her phone conversation, even though she hadn't.

"Now that you mention it, I could use a little something to eat," I said. "My treat."

"Sounds good," Alva Rose said, "since they don't offer any food during an inquisition."

Ouch. Guilt. Oh, horrible, punch-in-the-stomach guilt.

I only hoped that the girl in the white skirt was a clue to the mystery, and I could clear Alva Rose's name and all would be forgiven.

We settled in at a booth at the back. The air hung heavy with an overpowering but not unpleasant fried-fish aroma, tempting me, even though I wasn't all that hungry. But who in their right mind can say no to anything dropped in a deep fryer for a few minutes?

I glanced around. The place had a beach vibe, with walls decorated in *Endless Summer*-esque posters and such. It seems they tried to set the atmosphere with 60s music, but it was hard to hear over the clanging and banging noises echoing from the kitchen.

The waitress came by and took our Diet Coke orders. She rattled off the daily special— fried catfish with fries and coleslaw for a skoosh under ten dollars—and then left to get our drinks.

Before we could even look at the stained paper menus, a shadow fell across our table. I looked up to see the woman in the white denim skirt.

"Alva Rose?" she asked.

Alva Rose looked up. "Manda? Well I'll be a monkey's uncle! Sit! Sit! I was thinking how much I needed a good lawyer right now, and here you are!" Alva Rose scooted over on her bench seat and Manda slipped in beside her.

Could this be the same Manda who had dated Rusty in high school? What were the odds? She was about the right age. I looked at Tasha and Tasha looked at me. Coincidences like this never happened in my life. It was kind of cool when they did. We smiled.

Alva Rose introduced us all. "What are you doing back in town?" she asked Manda.

"I'm giving up the rat race in D.C. and moving back home. Got a great job lined up downtown, and signed a contract to build a cottage in that new upscale neighborhood on the bay."

"You go, girl," Alva Rose said as she high-fived Manda.

My phone dinged, indicating an incoming text. From Tasha. WE NEED TO FIND OUT WHAT MANDA KNOWS. SHE COULD BE OUR KILLER!

Great minds think alike!

When I looked up, I noticed Manda and Alva Rose involved in a deep conversation, heads almost touching as they spoke quickly and quietly. And animatedly. I leaned in, the better to hear what was being discussed.

"I heard you were in jail for T-Dub's murder," Manda said. "What a hoot! You! Killing anyone! But I'm glad to see you're out."

Alva Rose looked Manda right in the eyes. "I did kill him, and now I need your help. You game?"

The smile disappeared from Manda's face and her healthy blush faded straight to gray. Then she laughed. "Oh, you always were a great kidder, Alva Rose."

"Not kidding," Alva Rose said, her face all serious and sad.

"Not so fast," Tasha said, forcing her way into the conversation. "Before I go into details, Manda, are you in fact an attorney licensed in the state of Virginia?"

Manda nodded.

"And do you agree to represent Alva Rose, here, because she's gonna need to lawyer up right quick. She thinks she killed T-Dub, but we," Tasha indicated she and I together, "have information that she did not. But before we share what we know, we want to make sure the attorney-client privilege is in effect."

Manda nodded. "It would be my honor to represent my dear friend here." She patted Alva Rose's arm.

Over meals of Bay Burgers (hamburger patties topped with meaty Chesapeake Bay crab cakes) and a mountain of limp, greasy fries, we brought Manda up to speed on the events surrounding T-Dub's death. Then we brought Alva Rose up to speed on what we'd learned today and our belief that she had not killed T-Dub.

Tasha brought the elephant into the room as she pointed a ketchup-drenched French fry at Alva Rose and said, "I think you're covering for someone, and I think that someone is Rusty."

Alva Rose reeled back as if she'd been slapped across

the face by an invisible hand. "Never," she proclaimed. "Rusty didn't kill nobody. I did. I'm telling you, I clunked that rat bastard over the head with my frying pan."

"Then why did Rusty leave town that night, never to be heard from again? Hmmm?" Tasha asked in such a way that led me to believe she'd missed her calling as a prosecuting attorney.

Alva Rose looked Tasha right in the eyes and said, "Because he's a good son and helped me bury the body when asked. He didn't want to go to jail for helping me, though, so he high-tailed it outta town that night." Her upper lip trembled, and a lone tear made a crooked path down her cheek. "He left town to protect me."

Well, pin a tail on me and call me a donkey. This puts a whole new spin on my thinking, basically bringing me back to square one. I sat back and threw my napkin on the top of my empty plate.

"I think what we need at this point," Manda said, "is to submit the dead body for forensic testing."

"Brave words," Tasha said. "Because the other scenario we considered is that Alva Rose is covering for you." She shot a finger towards Manda.

Manda laughed heartily at that. "T-Dub may have been a miserable excuse for a human being, the way he sold drugs to school kids and all, but I can promise you I did not kill him."

"Stop the insanity." Alva Rose banged her hands against the table and rattled the flimsy silverware against the Formica table top. That got our attention. "I'm telling you I killed him and if they dig him up, then I've written myself a one-way ticket to the electric chair."

I had to admit, she had a point.

CHAPTER ELEVEN

Hollywood couldn't have staged a more perfect background for the morning's gruesome task. Gray skies and heavy clouds hung thick in the air. Wind-whipped waves crashed on the shore, slamming against the dunes behind Alva Rose's cottage and augmenting the atmosphere of gloom and despair. My heart was heavy as we prepared for the exhumation.

Manda had called in a favor of her friend Chris, who owns a septic tank business out in the rural part of Virginia. "Have Backhoe, Will Travel" proclaimed the advertisement on the side of his black F-350. Although he'd admitted he'd dug up many things, a dead body was not one of them.

Chris fired up the tractor and it roared to life. It puttered its way down the trailer's ramp and rumbled over towards the small garden that had been the first sign of life when I'd arrived in the neighborhood.

I now knew that garden to be the burial spot of Trent "T-Dub" Wiersteiner.

Alva Rose hadn't admitted in so many words, but when we'd dropped her off at home last night, she kept casting furtive glances towards the garden. That told us all we needed to know.

Manda now stood ringside, directing Chris where to dig. We all agreed that once we had evidence, we would call the police.

Tasha and I stood outside the white-picket fence with a front-row seat to the exhumation show.

The faded curtain at the window flickered. Alva Rose was watching, too.

I shivered against a gust of chilly breeze that caught me right at the nape of my neck and scooted under my t-shirt and down my back. I didn't want to run home to grab something warmer and risk not-seeing the main event. But I kind of/sort of did. I wasn't sure I had the stomach for seeing a decayed body pulled from the earth. How decayed a body buried for ten years would be I had no idea. There couldn't be much left . . .

The backhoe dug its teeth into the ground and began scraping.

Please don't let them find anything. I wanted more than anything for Alva Rose to just be old and crazy, and not a crazy old killer. That's me, ever the optimist, hoping for the best outcome given a bad situation.

The vegetables were gone within seconds. My thoughts drifted back to the tasty tomatoes Alva Rose and I had enjoyed with our burgers. Best I'd ever tasted. Could that have been on account of the minerals released during the decomposition of Trent's body? No, they would have sunk down, not up right? And it had been ten years. Still . . .

My attention was drawn back to the action when Manda raised her hand and yelled, "Halt." The backhoe idled.

Tasha leapt the fence in a single bound and took up position next to Manda. They stood shoulder-to-shoulder, staring at the ground.

"You thinking what I'm thinking?" Tasha asked loudly over the backhoe motor.

"That that bone looks like a human skull?" Manda responded.

Tasha nodded.

I glanced towards Alva Rose's cottage. The curtain had fallen back into place.

So now we had a skeleton and a confession. Slam dunk for the prosecution.

Personally, I didn't need to see any more of the tragedy to unfold, and I sure as heck didn't have the stomach to face Alva Rose right now. Head down, arms crossed, I skedaddled back to my little pink cottage. The place I thought would be my salvation had turned into my worst nightmare.

Thinking about Alva Rose murdering Trent Wiersteiner made me sad. Truth be told, it also had me a little bit freaked out. Make that a lot freaked out. I'd shared this lonely street of deserted houses with her. We'd shared dinner and wine and cupcakes. I could have done something to flip her killing switch at any time. I could have become the one pushing up tomatoes and pole beans from her garden. Who knew how many decades I would lay there before being excavated? It didn't bear thinking about.

It wasn't a conscious decision, I simply started packing my belongings, what few I had unpacked in the four days I'd called this beach cottage home. Time to tuck my tail between my legs and retreat to my safe secure Ohio town, where nobody had been murdered in the past 100 years, at least not to my knowledge.

The scene outside my window sent fingers of panic crawling up my spine. Seven black-and-whites and two other official looking vehicles had parked willy-nilly on the street. All kinds of uniformed folks wandered in an eerie sort of crime scene-investigation ballet.

As Dorothy said in *The Wizard of Oz*, "Toto, we're not in Kansas anymore."

Tasha came through the front door a few hours later. By then I had all the boxes stacked, ready for loading into my truck first thing tomorrow.

"What in the world is all this?" Tasha asked, glancing around.

"The sum total of everything I own in the world. Except for the hammock out back. I don't see how I'll fit it in my truck with all this other stuff. I'll leave it as a welcome gift to the new tenant." My shoulders sagged as I spoke. I hated to leave the hammock. Heck, I hated to leave this house, but there was no way I could stay.

"You're not leaving. You love it here," Tasha said. She really does know what goes on in my head. It's kind of scary sometimes.

"But I've been living near a murderer."

"Alva Rose isn't any more of a murderer than you or I."

"She's not?"

"No. I think she is suffering from delusions of murder, and maybe over the years has convinced herself she killed T-Dub." Tasha pulled the folded card table away from the wall and set it back up in the dining room. Then she grabbed two folding chairs and set them up also. "Sit," she ordered.

I sat. "What's your theory, then?"

"First, her motive is weak. Seriously, what kind of woman kills someone because they are romantic competition for their son? A grown son, at that? You only hear that kind of crazy talk from stage moms. Does Alva Rose strike you as a stage mom?"

Calling up a mental picture of tiny Alva Rose with her blue curls and the fashion-sense of a bag lady, I had to agree. Definitely not stage-mom material.

"And then," Tasha talked as she walked into the kitchen, her voice rising as she got further away from me, "the phone call you overheard by Brooke. I'm thinking somebody got to Trent first, and Alva Rose whacked an already dead guy on the head. Do you really think that ninety-pound-dripping-wet woman could hit someone hard enough to kill them?"

Of course she couldn't. She'd barely been able to lift a pint-sized glass of Lancaster Lemonade. It seemed so obvious, now. Why hadn't we thought of it earlier? Oh yeah, because we were not well versed in the fine art of cracking murder mysteries.

"My theory is backed up by the forensics guy out there. He did a preliminary examination of the skull and didn't find any evidence of blunt force trauma. His words, not mine. If Alva Rose had hit him hard enough to kill him, the skull would have shown a fracture or something."

Hmmm. Now that was interesting. A ray of hope for my death-row condemned neighbor.

Tasha returned to the dining cove with a box of half-eaten Wheat Thins and a tub of Boursin Garlic and Fine Herbs Cheese. We both dug in like we hadn't eaten all day. Which, come to think on it, we hadn't.

"How would an already dead Trent come to be on Alva Rose's sofa then?" I asked around a mouth full of cheese and crackers.

Tasha slipped into the chair across from me. "That, my friend, is the sixty-four-thousand-dollar question, and you and I are going to find the answer."

"And how do you propose we do that?"

"I'm still working out the details, but it involves us getting our hands-on Brooke's phone and seeing what number she called yesterday when you overheard her conversation. You up for another night at Betty's Beach Bar?"

I shrugged. It's not like I had anything else on my social calendar.

"Eat up, then," she said, pushing the tub of cheese towards me.

I used the last cracker to scrape the last globs of cheese from the side of the container. "I would like nothing more than to prove Alva Rose is innocent."

"I'm sure she'd like that, too. She's over there telling any cop who will listen that she killed him. Time for us to put our Snoop Sister skills to the test. Go get dressed, Gwendolyn."

"Ready in five, Ernesto." My heart raced a little bit at the promise of solving this ten-year-old crime and saving Alva Rose from the electric chair. I hadn't played the role of heroine since, well, forever. Maybe Tasha was onto something here, forging a new career as a crime-fighting super hero. I could do that. I could get my PI's license and become a real-life Nancy Drew. Wouldn't that send my ex into a tailspin?

But the little voice inside my head whispered to me words of caution, those of my grandmother's old Haitian proverb: THE CRAB THAT WALKS TOO FAR, FALLS INTO THE POT.

CHAPTER TWELVE

Never in all my years have I seen so many people crammed into a drinking establishment. Live music, courtesy of a very talented band, belted out "Brown-Eyed Girl." People shimmied and shook in the aisles. At the "Sha-la-la dee dah" part, everyone, to include bartenders, shouted along. The atmosphere was contagious and I shouted along with the rest of them. Gawd, I enjoyed being part of this energy. Made me feel like a teenager again. A girl could get used to this kind of fun on a Friday night. Sure beats sitting home alone watching old Marilyn Monroe movies.

I found a small space to stand and observe while Tasha went in search of refreshments. I had a good view of the dance floor, and also the corridor leading to the Little Gulls room. We had a goal—get our hands on Brooke's cell phone—but didn't have a plan. Yet.

Tasha returned with drinks, hurricane glasses filled with an orange liquid. "Orange Crush," she yelled to me as she handed the colorful libation.

One sip and I was hooked. An Orange Crush turned out to be a delightful mix of fresh squeezed orange juice, orange-flavored vodka and triple sec, served over crushed ice. At the risk of repeating myself, a girl could get used to this kind of Friday-night fun.

Conversation was impossible. We watched the dancers, swaying to the music, and enjoying our citrusy libations.

We were a few rounds in when Tasha jostled my

elbow. I managed not to spill a single drop. I turned to give her my *It's a crime to waste alcohol* look. She nodded agreement, then tipped her head towards the hallway. I looked that way. Brooke was sashaying down the hall.

Crap! The drinks had gone to my legs, and it was a challenge to walk, let alone out maneuver someone who had recently arrived. I didn't want to do this.

"Come on," Tasha yelled in my ear.

I didn't think I could get my legs to go, but I couldn't send my best friend in alone. We were a team. The Snoop Sisters.

With a nod between us, we put OPERATION: GET BROOK'S CONTACT LIST into action.

Lucky us. We lined up right behind Brook in the rather long line to the restroom, which I knew from experience could accommodate only two women at a time. A real design flaw if you ask me.

While a little bit quieter away from the bar, it was still too noisy to talk. Brooke wasn't talking anyway, she was scrolling through text messages on her phone.

According to my calculations, we had at least seven minutes to put our plan into action. Well technically we had to come up with a plan first, and then put it to action. My mind spun its wheels a mile a minute, but came up with nothing. *Think! Think! Think!*

"Gawd, I love this song," Brooke said to us, moving her feet and wiggling her hips to the beat of "Be Young, Be Foolish, Be Happy."

"Me too," Tasha said, wiggling along. But I noticed her gaze never left Brooke's phone.

"If you're in a hurry to get back to the dance floor I'll watch the door for you." I nodded towards the Little Buoys room. "I haven't seen anyone come or go since we've been in line."

"Wow," Brooke said. "Thanks." She started to slip her phone in the back pocket of her tight jeans, then realized the style had no back pocket. She looked at me, then the phone. "Here, hold my phone." She handed the latest iPhone to me. "There's no place in there I'd want to put it down. I'll be real quick, I promise."

And just like that, we had Brooke's phone. Being an Android user, I handed it off to Tasha, then I slipped over and stood watch by the door, positioning myself so that I could hear when she was finishing up her business in order to send a warning motion to my partner in crime solving.

Tasha went to work.

The seconds ticked by slower than a snail traveling through peanut butter.

Brooke's phone rang. I looked at Tasha. Tasha looked at me. Then she answered the call.

OH MY GAWD! Is it a federal offense to answer someone else's phone?

I heard the toilet flush, and made a hurry up motion to Tasha.

She was listening to the person on the other end of the line. Her face had taken on a horror-stricken look.

Oh, this wasn't good. Not at all.

The sound of water running and splashing, then the hand dryer. My "hurry up" motions became frantic.

The sound of high heels on the tile floor approached the door. I couldn't help it, I squealed. I was *soooo* not cut out for investigative work!

Tasha dropped the phone by her side and gave me a thumbs up.

Mission accomplished.

Woosh. The door flew open. I stepped to the side. "Nobody got by on my watch," I said and smiled.

Tasha handed the phone over.

"Thanks," Brooke said, then shag-stepped her way down the hallway and back to the dance floor.

Tasha grabbed me by the arm and we rushed outside to the fresh, cool air.

"Who called?" I asked. "And why do you look like you just saw Aunt Ruth's ghost?"

"You won't believe this." Tasha began pacing the parking lot, running her fingers through her hair. I'd never seen this kind of behavior in her, and frankly, it scared the beejezus out of me. "The guy thought I was Brooke, and told me he's gonna take care of things once and for all. He couldn't risk the identity of T-Dub's killer getting revealed. Only he didn't put it quite that nicely."

"You think he killed T-Dub?"

"No doubt in my mind." Tasha's hands shook as she wiped perspiration from her upper lip.

"You think 'taking care of things once and for all' means he's gonna kill Brooke?"

Tasha nodded. "If you heard the venom in his voice, you would know he was serious."

"Any idea who it was?"

"Caller ID said Frank Franklin."

"Frank Franklin, the Furniture Czar? He's the guy with the obnoxious commercials." I thought about that for a second and something Alva Rose told me clicked. "And he grew up on Waters Edge. Two doors down from Alva Rose. It's not a big stretch to think of him paling around with Brooke and Trent."

"But what do we have as a motive?"

"Could be anything."

We stood under a parking lot light, each lost in our own guesses as to what role the Furniture Czar could have played in the murder.

"Should we tell Brooke?" I asked. "Or would it be better to go straight to the police?"

Headlights swept across us. The sound of tires crunching through the oyster-shell parking echoed in the night. I turned towards the noise. A sleek black Porsche eased up to the front door of Betty's Beach Bar and parked in the handicap spot, even though he did not display the proper disabled parking pass.

The license plate confirmed my worst fear, F CZAR.

He had his window open. Lights from the bar enabled us to see the driver.

"It's Frank Franklin," Tasha said, her voice tinged with terror.

"How do you know that?"

She showed me a picture on her phone, an ad for Frank Franklin, The Furniture Czar.

"Come on." Tasha started walking towards the car.

"Wait! What do you think you're doing?"

"I need to hear his voice. Could have been somebody else using his phone."

I had a bad feeling about this. Really bad.

I watched as Tasha marched right up to the car and began chatting the man up. I sidled close enough to hear, but far enough away I could dial nine-one-one if need be.

The Czar took inventory of Tasha's physical attributes.

"I'm staying with my friend on Waters Edge," Tasha said in a flirty voice.

Fatal mistake number one: never tell a suspected killer where you live.

"There was a murder there about ten years ago," Tasha said.

Fatal mistake number two: never bait a killer into a confession.

"What's that got to do with me?" Frank snarled.

I'd never actually heard evil in a person's voice until that moment. It scared me down to my toes.

Brooke walked out of the front door of the bar. She was alone, head bowed, looking at her phone.

"Hi, Brooke," Tasha called.

Brooke looked up at Tasha. Her gaze slipped to the Porsche. Fear crept across her face the way it does in slow-motion horror movies. She mouthed a very bad word and then turned and ran through the parking lot.

Frank revved the Porsche's engine. "That bitch! I'm gonna kill her." His high-performance sports car jumped backwards out of the parking spot. It rolled a few feet then shot forward, tires spinning on the oyster shell parking lot.

Did Frank Franklin plan to mow down Brooke, squishing her flatter than a grape under a steamroller? It seemed that way.

I couldn't give him the chance. My protective-momma-bear instincts kicked in and the next thing I knew I was running, then jumping, towards the car. *Thump!* I landed on the hood of the accelerating vehicle as it sped down a row of parked cars. My fingers wrapped around the lip of the hood where it butted up to the wiper blades. The dashboard lights illuminated the face of a crazed man who seemed hell-bent on making sure someone wouldn't live long enough to see another sunrise.

It was quite possible that someone would be me . . .

One row over, an engine roared to life and the sound of another car's tires crunching oyster shells could be heard. *Please let that be Brooke.* If I could distract Frank for a few more seconds, she'd get away.

"Get off my car, bitch" he yelled as he swerved left to right to left, trying to shake me off the way a dog shakes off soap suds. I held on tight, but I knew I couldn't for much longer. My body swung left, then right, then left, like a pendulum on a grandfather clock.

The Porsche reached the road. The engine rumbled beneath me, and the car sped up, still swerving back and forth across the pavement.

I held on for dear life, literally.

One strong swerve left and I slid off the hood, landing in the grassy space between the road and the sidewalk. The pain was immediate and nauseating. From the tip of my head to the heels of my feet, it felt like every bone in my body had broken.

Not far off in the distance, I heard a tremendous crash, the sound of metal twisting and glass breaking, followed by a long and mournful wail.

I wouldn't know until the next day that was the last noise Frank Franklin would ever make.

CHAPTER THIRTEEN

Life Lesson #1734. . .
Never agree to solve a murder with your friend,
no matter how good of a friend she is.

I could have been killed," I said to Tasha as I laid on my hospital bed. Fortunately, I hadn't broken *every* bone in my body, just four of them.

"But you weren't." Tasha tipped a straw for me to take a few nips of the contraband Starbucks coffee she'd brought me.

I took a few swallows and then relaxed back into the pillows. It hurt to sip. Heck, it hurt to breathe. According to the doctor, I had three broken ribs, a cracked collar bone, a contusion on my head, and a really, really, really sore back due to muscle strain. I had no memory of crashing into a fire hydrant when I'd been flung from the speeding Porsche, but apparently that's what happened. I'm glad I fell off when I did. I doubt I would have survived a higher speed. And I know I wouldn't have survived the crash.

I let my eyelids drift closed. All I could see was the memory of Frank's Porsche smashed against the concrete utility pole. He'd lost control of the car after I'd fallen off, then smashed head-on, into a structure designed to withstand Cat-5 hurricane winds. His Porsche hadn't stood a chance. "I'm responsible for his death," I whispered to myself. If I hadn't jumped on his car, he'd still be alive.

"No," Tasha said, once again reading my mind.

"Frank is responsible for his own death. He should have never tried to swing you off his car." She pulled the thin, scratchy blankets up to my chin, and then slipped her hands into mine and squeezed. "I don't mind telling you, I saw your life flash before my eyes."

I managed a weak smile.

"You are a hero, you know. You saved Brooke's life."

My battered, bruised, and broken body didn't feel very heroic. It felt stupid. Thomas Magnum of TV-series fame had made killer-chasing look so easy. Of course, he'd had a stunt double.

Forget this detecting business. My ex was right, I am not cut out for adventure.

There came a knock on the door and I turned my head ever so slightly, but enough to send pain shooting down my arm. Broken ribs are not for sissies.

"Come in," Tasha called.

The door cracked and Brooke poked her head through. She held a beautiful bouquet of lilies in her arms. "Hi, it's me."

I wasn't sure who I was expecting, but not Brooke.

Tasha gave my hands a final squeeze then pulled away. "We were just talking about you."

Brooke seemed unsure of herself as she inched her way towards my bedside. She placed the flowers on the stand by the window, and then turned and approached my bed. "I really don't know how to thank you. I understand you distracted Frank long enough for me to get away. You saved my life. He always said he would kill me one day, and it seems that day had come."

"Why?" I asked.

"Because I knew he was the one who'd killed Trent. I'd been with him that night."

Eventually we got the full story out of Brooke.

Trent had been drug dealer. He'd started out selling alcohol to high school kids but it hadn't been long before he moved on to marijuana, then harder drugs. Two classmates of Brooke's had overdosed and died, but the police couldn't build a case against him. Brooke hated her brother for what he'd done, but he bought her silence with nice clothes and a red Mazda convertible for her 16th birthday. When her best friend Cindy Franklin—Frank Franklin's baby sister—had attended one of Trent's Famous Rager parties, she'd mixed what turned out to be a lethal combination of alcohol and cocaine.

The story retelling stopped for a good five minutes here while Brooke cried and Tasha comforted. It was all I could do to not tell her to knock it off and get on with the story. What I really wanted to do was close my eyes and sleep and escape from the pain coursing through my body.

Eventually Brooke got her emotions under control and resumed the telling.

"One night I followed Trent, camera in hand. I'd hoped to take pictures of him dealing drugs and give evidence to the police. I wanted nothing more than for him to be locked away for the rest of his life so that he couldn't kill any more of my friends.

"The first stop on his route that night was Alva Rose's house. Well, it was Rusty's house, too, at the time. I figured that's who he was meeting, although I'd never heard of Rusty being into the drug scene. T-Dub knocked on the door. When no one answered, he turned the knob and walked in. I snuck around to all the windows hoping to get a view of the transaction, but all the drapes were drawn so I couldn't see a thing. I very quietly snuck through the front door and spotted T-Dub sitting on the sofa, watching TV, waiting for Rusty. I slipped into the coat closet, and with the door ajar, had a good view of the living room.

"Footsteps in the hall let me know Rusty was home, only the person who walked into the living room wasn't Rusty, but Frank. He still lived down the street. He hadn't made it big in business yet. He sat down next to T-Dub, they chatted a bit, more like gossiped. I thought it was all very civil considering Frank knew T-Dub had supplied Cindy the stuff that had killed her.

"Frank pulled a cellophane-wrapped brownie out of

his shirt pocket. He opened it and started to take a bite. T-Dub grabbed it out of Trent's hands and ate the whole thing in one bite. He'd always been a glutton for chocolate. Turns out Frank counted on that."

Brooke stood and paced the small room, her arms wrapped tight across her mid-section. She drew a deep breath and continued. "They sat back and watched TV together. T-Dub fell asleep. That was unusual. That brother of mine never slept. Not that I saw, anyway. I think it was his guilty conscience. That was my first clue that something was wrong. Then I watched Frank reach over and take his pulse. He nodded his head and smiled. Looked like The Grinch himself when he stole Christmas.

"Frank left, whistling a happy tune as he strolled out the door. I raced to my brother, but I couldn't find a pulse, either." Brooke hung her head.

The only noise I heard was nurse's shoes squeaking on the floor outside my hospital door.

"Frank came back. When he saw me, he yelled, 'How long you been here?' " Brooke rubbed her hands down her thighs, took a deep breath and looked back up at us.

Tasha nodded, encouraging Brooke to continue the story.

She did. "I pleaded with Frank to help my brother, but Frank just looked at me. 'If you ever tell anyone about this, I will kill you, too. And that's a promise.' " Brooke choked on her sobs.

Tasha wrapped her arm around Brooke. It seemed cruel and unusual punishment to make the girl relive the horrors of that night when she was a teenager. But we, the collective society of we, needed to know the full story.

Brooke scrubbed the tears off her face, and then drew a deep breath. When she spoke again, it was barely above a whisper. "He dragged me out of the house and watched until I went inside my home. I cried and cried, but never told anyone. T-Dub's body was never found. I never knew what Frank did with it." Her shoulders slumped. "I can't believe Alva Rose thought she'd killed him. All those years she held on to that secret."

"But someone knew," Tasha said. "Sydney overheard your phone conversation when you said, 'If she overheard, I'm a dead woman,' referring to Manda."

Brooke nodded. "Manda always suspected I knew something about T-Dub's death. If she knew I knew something she would drill me like a hostile witness until I cracked. But Frank would never let that happen. He'd kill me first." Brooke's tears began again, in earnest.

Tasha could handle them. All I wanted to do was close my eyes and sleep. Just a little nap.

When I woke up, Alva Rose was there watching me, her blue-curls blowing ever so slightly under the air conditioning vent. She had her hands together as if in prayer.

"Thank you," she said, then started crying.

Another person entered the room, a tall, husky man with reddish-brown hair. "Is she awake?" he asked.

Alva Rose nodded.

"I'm Rusty Llewellyn," he said, proffering his hand.

Alva Rose's son had returned. "Nice to meet you," I said, "And I'd shake your hand if I could move."

"Of course," he said, and tucked his hand in his pocket. "I wanted to thank you. Tasha told me you'd been the one to call. Mom's filled me in on what you did for her. I really appreciate it. It's nice to know after all these years that she didn't kill T-Dub. I've been dealing with the guilt, as has she. All for nothing."

The door opened and in walked Tasha and Manda, chatting like two BFFs. It's a good thing I'm not the jealous type. And that I was the hungry type. Tasha held the biggest pizza box I had ever seen, and in it my favorite mushroom, chicken and onion pizza pie. Soon the room was filled with the wonderful aromas which overpowered the antiseptic hospital smell. We swapped stories about what had happened the last few days.

The atmosphere buzzed with hope and forgiveness. Rusty and Manda held hands and caught up. I got the feeling Lina was no longer in the picture. But if not, who was I to judge?

Alva Rose sat on the side chair, her gaze darting between the reunited lovebirds and the bandaged-up me. Tasha perched on my bed, texting on her phone what I would later learn to be a full account of our adventures. She parlayed the story into a book deal. My share of the proceeds allowed me to purchase the little pink cottage by the sea. It's where I hang my flip flops. It's my home.

THE END

DOWN BY THE BAY

"Down by the Bay" asks the question, "Can you have a future if you can't remember the past?" When Skye Whitmore is shown a picture of a seaside house, she has fuzzy memories of living there as a young girl and recalls moments spent gardening or reading with her mother. Upon learning that the house is where her mother died, darker memories bubble to the surface but fail to assemble into a complete picture. With more questions than answers, she sets off to find out what exactly happened in that house thirty years ago.

CHAPTER ONE

You're not gonna believe what happened to Mudge!"

That's just like Libby Abernathy, my randomly assigned college roommate at the University of Virginia and my BFF for the seventeen years hence, to get right to the point. No small talk for that girl.

Snuggling my iPhone up to my ear, I continued pushing my cart down the frozen food aisle of my local Piggly Wiggly. As I passed by the pizza section, I reached into the freezer bin and pulled out two Stouffer's Deluxe French Bread pizzas, my favorite go-to choice for a "home-cooked" meal. Hey, if I have to turn the oven on, then it's "home-cooked" in my book.

"Go on, guess," Libby said.

"Knowing Mudge, it could be anything." Mudge, whose real name was Marcus Lee Abernathy III, was Libby's husband, and the total opposite of what you might think a "Mudge" would look like.

"So you give up?"

"Yup." I added a Stouffer's family size stuffed green peppers to my basket for the next time I felt like "cooking."

"Mudge's Aunt Alice died," Libby said.

I stopped my cart and let the news process. "My condolences on his loss." I'd known Mudge as long as I'd known Libby, had attended many of their family parties, and was an honorary member of the Abernathy clan. I tried to invoke an image of Aunt Alice, but nothing came to mind. "Wait, which one is Aunt Alice?"

"You don't know her because she's from the Patterson side and lives down North Carolina way. His grandmother and Alice were half-sisters. Turns out Mudge was her only surviving relative, and even though the last time he saw her was back in eighty-three when he spent a summer down there, she left all her worldly belongings to him. She actually died last June but he's just hearing about it—"

Two small beeps indicated I had an incoming call. I checked the screen. My twelve-year-old son, Blake. Cue the impending doom music.

"Hey Libby," I said. "That's Blake ringing in. He's only supposed to call me if it's an emergency. Gotta run."

"I hope everything's okay. Call me back."

"Will do. Love ya." I connected over to the incoming call, my stomach doing flipflops while I imagined what emergency situation had arisen. "Blake?"

"Mom? The dogs are puking their guts out, and I don't know what to do."

I sighed. Emergency is in the eye of the beholder. "Clean it up and I'll be home as soon as I can."

"I'm not touching it." The tone of voice made it clear that no amount of cajoling or bribery would get him to change his mind. It's been my experience that the willingness to perform those "gross" types of tasks is a double-X chromosome trait.

"Well, do something." I thought about the white carpet in the quaint Cape Codder we'd moved into last week. The house had come with wall-to-wall Saxony the color of a polar bear, because don't think for a second I'm the type of woman who's delusional and thinks it would stay white for more than a day, what with two dogs and a boy who'd never met a puddle he didn't think needed stomping through. So far it still looked decent, but if the dog-vomit stains weren't cleaned up quickly and properly, it would mean new flooring. And that wasn't in the budget right now. "I'm on my way."

I abandoned my half-filled grocery cart and raced out

the door. As I sped along the snowy streets of Gloucester, Virginia, the conversation with Blake niggled at my worry button. Had that been a note of hysteria in his voice? And a curious thought: Banshee and Bella-Boo, our precious pound puppies, had never gotten sick like that before. I dug my phone out of my purse and called him back. "How're you doing?" I asked.

"Fine."

"Did you get everything cleaned up?"

"I turned trashcans over it so I don't have to look at it."

I sighed. If all of life's problems could be solved so easily. "Any idea what made the dogs so sick?"

"Probably because they licked up some of the fire extinguisher stuff."

"Fire extinguisher stuff?"

"Yeah. I had to put out a fire."

"What fire?" My foot pressed the accelerator to the floorboard. The whine of the engine almost drowned out the sound of my heart hammering in my chest. Almost.

"The fire in the oven," Blake explained, as if it were an everyday event. "One of the chicken nuggets slid off the pan and burst into flames. But don't worry. I put it out so the house didn't burn down or anything."

I made the final turn onto Poplar Lane and spotted my little white house at the end of the cul-de-sac. Nary a smoke tendril curled out of the dormer windows. I offered up a quick *Thank you, God.*

After parking my aging Dodge Caravan at the curb, I sat a few minutes while my heartbeat slowed and my trembling hands stilled. Everything was fine.

Or not, as I soon learned.

While the house hadn't burned to a crisp, there was a lot of collateral damage. All across my white house (yes, the previous owner had a white fetish) a layer of fine, yellow powder covered everything. Like a dusting of snow, the contents from the fire extinguisher had floated throughout the rooms settled on every surface available:

floor, shoe molding, baseboards, sofas, chairs, tables, lamp shades, books. Everywhere there was a horizontal surface, there was yellow powder. I navigated my way around the upended trashcans leading to the kitchen.

The dogs scratched at the back door and yipped to be let in, but I didn't want them walking through this mess and getting sick again. Not until I—make that we— conducted a thorough housecleaning. The exact thing I did *not* want to do right now.

Blake came and stood next to me by the oven, the yellow powder crunching against the white tile floor as he walked.

Ruffling my fingers through his curly blond hair, I reminded myself that in the grand scheme of things, a little (okay, a lot) of overspray from the fire extinguisher was a small price to pay for still having a house. My heart started pounding again at the mere thought of everything I held dear going up in smoke. Something about fires—or even the mere possibility of one—scared the beejezus out of me. I had no explanation why, though. Maybe something devastating had happened to me in a previous life. Not that I believe in past life regression or anything, but really, what other explanation is there for my innate fear of house fires?

I drew three calming breaths. "So, how big was this fire?" I asked my son.

"There were flames all over the bottom of the oven," Blake said.

"Really?" In all my years of having nuggets or fries fall off the cookie sheet, I had never had one erupt into flames. Usually they baked into charcoal and laid like black lava rocks until I wiped them up.

I opened the oven and peered inside. More pale-yellow powder, but no charcoal nuggets.

A thought hit me. I closed the door and turned the gas oven on, then opened it again. Cooking flames made a U around the bottom of the oven. "Is this the fire you saw?"

"Holy crap!" Blake turned and raced for the fire extinguisher on the kitchen table.

"Wait." I shut the oven door and turned it off. I didn't know whether to laugh or scream or shake some common sense into him. My son, who had only ever cooked with an electric oven, had extinguished the flames in our new home's gas oven.

Before I could set Blake straight on the facts of cooking life, the doorbell rang. The door opened. "Yoo-hoo," a familiar voice called out. Moments later, Libby appeared in the kitchen, looking fabulous, as always. *All designer, all the time*, was her motto, even when dancing Zumba at the local gym. Today she looked like she'd been shopping on Rodeo Drive, but had probably only been down to the JCP at the Towne Mall.

"What the hell happened here?" She gave Blake a hug and opened the door to let Banshee and Bella-Boo in. Yipping and yapping and general chaos ensued before Blake got the dogs leashed up and off on a walk around the block.

"You look like you could use a glass of wine, sugar," Libby said. "Have you unpacked the corkscrew yet?"

"Hand carried it from the old house to the new. Top drawer, left of the sink."

"I'll pour while you sit and look at this." She handed me her iPhone. "That's what Mudge inherited from Aunt Alice."

On the iPhone was a picture of a white clapboard, three-story monstrosity perched above a bay. Rows of pink peonies lined a long sidewalk that led up to a pale-blue front door.

A cold feeling spread slowly through my veins, as if someone had hooked me up to a Slushee IV.

I knew that house . . .

CHAPTER TWO

I sat down—hard—on a kitchen chair. It tipped backwards, and I felt myself suspended at the point between falling over and settling down on all four legs.

Libby shoved me forward while simultaneously sliding a goblet of merlot under my nose. "Drink," she ordered.

I took a long, nerve-calming sip. Well, maybe more of a gulp. It was, after all, medicinal.

"Talk," she said as she pulled a chair closer to mine and sat.

Oh, how to explain. The memories of that house were vague, but I knew without a shadow of a doubt that was the house I'd lived in as a child. It had been back when my mother was still alive, so before my fifth birthday. I picked up Libby's iPhone again and stared at the picture. "Where is this house?" I asked.

"Hutchins, North Carolina. It's a small town on the Albemarle Sound."

That didn't ring a bell, but then again, I'd only been four-years old. "Any idea what street it's on?"

"Periwinkle Place. Crazy name, huh?"

That icy feeling spread through my veins again as a memory seeped into the conscious portion of my mind. A memory of my mother's voice, soft and kind, as she holds me in her arms and speaks to me. *See this purple flower here, Skye? It's a Periwinkle. We live on Periwinkle Place. Someday I'm going to fill our entire garden with these pretty flowers.*

She never got the chance, because shortly after that she'd died.

"Drink some more wine," Libby said. "You're looking like you're going to pass out. Or puke. I'm not real keen on either option."

I wasn't either, so I took a sip of the merlot and let the memory replay another time in my head.

Crackers and cheese appeared on the table, and after a few nibbles and a couple more sips of the nectar of the gods, I started feeling more myself.

"Ready to talk yet?" Libby asked.

"Not much to say." I shrugged. "I lived in that house with my mom, and I'm pretty sure that's where she suffered a fatal head injury when she fell. Since my father was focused on his naval career, he'd hustled me out of there and dropped me off with Aunt Martha. And you know how that went." Libby had heard all my Mean Old Aunt Martha stories during our roommate days back at the University of Virginia.

Looking at the picture summoned feelings of anger and abandonment that my adult self had *almost* succeeded in repressing. Those feelings hit me full-force right now, and I got angry all over again. No young child should be dumped off with a distant relative, let alone a cranky one who lived in a dingy, isolated cabin in the mountains of western Virginia. It's the stuff that bestselling memoirs are made of. Those heart-wrenching ones that require at least one box of Kleenex to get through.

Right now, the only therapy I had available was in my wine glass. I took a sip, and then picked up Libby's iPhone and looked at the picture again.

Seeing the house on Periwinkle Place evoked memories of a much more loving and nurturing environment. I sipped/gulped more wine. The dulcet tones of my mother's singing voice filled my head: *Down by the bay, where the watermelons grow . . .*

Libby rubbed my forearm. "You okay, sugar?"

"It's a shock, seeing it again after all these years."

"I can imagine." Libby pushed her glass to the center of the table. "What are the odds that out of all the gazillions of houses in this world, the one Mudge inherits is the one where you lived as a kid? Un-effing-believable." She brushed some of the fire-extinguisher powder off of the table, and then wiped her hands on her DKNY slacks. "Hey, what happened here anyway?"

I drained my goblet then gave her the Cliff's Notes' version of Blake's after-school snack preparation. Libby laughed so hard she started to cry.

With a refilled glass, I settled back in my chair and sipped while waiting for her guffaws to subside. I used the time to contemplate the reality of the gargantuan cleaning tasks ahead of me. It was going to be a long night.

Libby wiped her eyes. "I gotta take Blake's side on this one," she said. "You get three bad-momma demerits for not conducting Gas Oven 101 class before leaving him alone to cook."

Did I ever mention that I love Libby to death, but I hate her when she's right?

The garage door slammed and in rushed Blake.

"Leave the dogs out, please," I called.

He complied, leaving them in the garage where they yipped to be let in. Blake made a bee-line for the refrigerator. He opened it and peered inside. "There's never anything to eat in this house." He slammed the door shut then went for the snack cabinet, pulling out a bag of pretzel M&Ms.

"Don't fill up on junk," I said. "Give me five more minutes with Libby then I'll call for pizza. Until it gets here, why don't you grab the vacuum and start cleaning up this mess?"

"Why do I have to do it?" He spoke in that whiney tone that always seemed to grate on my last nerve. It was especially grating this afternoon.

"Because you made it," I responded through teeth clenched tightly together.

"My cue to exit stage right." Libby grabbed her iPhone off the table and tucked it in her pocket. She gave me and Blake each a hug goodbye then my Jimmy Choo-wearing friend crunched her way across the powder-y floor and then out the front door.

After Blake and I shared a ham and pineapple pizza, I made Blake help me clean up the mess. And boy, what a mess. It took us until three o'clock in the morning. The longer we cleaned, the fussier I got. When we were finally done, I dropped a goodnight kiss on the top of his head as I do every night. The tired woman in me couldn't let him go without one snarky comment. "I hope you learned your lesson about using the fire extinguisher."

"I did," he sniped back. "Next time I'm gonna let the house burn down."

Sigh. Whoever it was that said "Parenting ain't for sissies" wasn't kidding.

I took myself off to bed and snuggled deep under the eider-down quilt. I was comfy, cozy and bone-deep exhausted. You'd think I'd have fallen right to sleep. But I didn't. I tossed and turned as the picture of the house Libby had shown me kept flashing in my mind like a damned neon sign. There was something behind that blue door. Something had happened, something which had deeply affected my childhood, and hence my teenage-hood and adulthood. Something so terrible I had obviously repressed it. Seeing that picture had me curious to find out what secrets lurked behind that blue door.

Curious, but totally freaked-out, too.

CHAPTER THREE

From that night on, my dreams were haunted by spooky swirly images of that blue door on the house on Periwinkle Place. I'd wake up more exhausted than when I'd first closed my eyes. And while my appetite decreased, my thirst for merlot increased. I became a functioning zombie. Okay, a slightly tipsy functioning zombie, but I managed to hang on to my job as a real estate agent. Thank goodness the market was on the slow side right now.

Reality check: I needed some answers and I needed them before my liver gave out. There was one person in this world who might have answers. That someone would be my father, Stephen George Crenshaw, III.

A quick Google search found him living in Tampa, Florida, now retired from the Navy. Did I want to see him? No. Could I have called him and asked the questions? Yes. But my little voice told me the kind of questions I had required a look into his eyes to make sure I was getting the truth, the whole truth and nothing but the truth. Besides, I hadn't seen my dad in over twenty years. It was time.

The President's Day holiday was at hand. Blake and I could fly to Tampa, do a pop-in at Dad's house, ask a few burning questions, go dip our toes in the Gulf of Mexico and then fly back home. A nice little fun-in-the-sun, shake-off-the-winter-blues trip for us that was doable on a tight budget. And then, maybe once I'd asked Dad what was behind the blue door, that little demon voice in the back of my head would be quieted and I could get some rest.

That evening, while serving Blake my second-favorite

low-effort home-cooked dinner (chocolate-chip pancakes drenched in Vermont maple syrup with a side of crisp bacon), I ever-so-casually asked, "Hey, how would you like to go visit your grandpa?"

"When did I get a grandpa?" Blake asked.

"You've always had one. I just wasn't very good about keeping in touch with him." Truth be told, I'd lost all contact with my father after the last college tuition bill had been paid. During my days as a student, our communication had been made exclusively through the ATM machine. Dad had probably been thrilled to be relieved of my financial demands, and I'd been thrilled to be relieved of his pseudo-emotional ones. I'd never told him I'd gotten married and divorced, let alone had a son who was now twelve-years old.

"You have a dad?" Blake asked.

"Of course."

"And I have a grandpa?"

"Yup," I said. An answer much too short for the question he'd asked.

"Cool. I can't wait to tell Jason that I have a grandpa, too. He's always bragging about his."

Yeah, I probably should have said something earlier. Sometimes I wish there were do-overs in life.

"Do I have a grandma, too?"

"No, she died when I was very young."

"Oh." Blake shoved a forkful of pancakes into his mouth, chewed thoughtfully, then asked, "What's my grandpa like?"

I sat down on the table next to my son and answered the question to the best of my memory. "He's tall, and blond-haired, like you. He spent most of his life in the Navy."

"Has he ever killed a pirate?"

"You'll have to ask him."

The stream of questions continued through dinner and while packing the few things we'd need for the weekend. Ninety-nine percent of my answers were, "You'll have to ask him." Not because I was too tired to explain, but because I honestly didn't know the answers. Kind of sad, huh?

We boarded a plane at 6:05 the next morning.

Four-and-a-half hours later we were standing on the steps of my father's Spanish-style casa in a neighborhood of cookie-cutter casas, each with one gently swaying palm tree smack dab in the middle of the front yard. My legs were about as strong as wet noodles, and I thought I might melt into a puddle right there on the front stoop. Were it not for Blake tucked under my arm, I would have turned tail and run all the way back to Virginia.

That actually sounded like a good idea.

As I turned to make my escape, Blake reached out his finger and pressed the doorbell.

I heard footsteps on the other side of the door. Too late now.

A tug at the sheer curtains covering the side window caught my attention. A second later the door opened. For the first time in my adult life, I stood face to face with my father. He wore a plaid shirt, jeans and high-mileage running shoes. Other than the telltale signs of age, he looked exactly as I remembered him. Maybe I remembered him that way because he looked so much like Blake. I felt a tiny tug at my heartstrings and that weak-kneed feeling returned three-fold. I pulled Blake a bit closer and leaned on him because I really felt like I was about to tipple right over.

"Skye?" my father asked.

I nodded. Slowly. My mouth wasn't working. I couldn't even form the word "Hello." And then, all of a sudden, it started working. "What can you tell me about the house with the blue door?"

He took a step back as if I'd sucker punched him, and his face lost the little bit of color it had. I wish I could take back those words and rephrase them a little. Okay, a lot. But in my defense, I'd asked him that very question at least a thousand times in my mind. I'd never let my imagination go far enough to think about his reaction, though. He looked like he was about to pass out.

A woman walked up behind Dad. She was tall and had long, silky brown hair pulled over her left shoulder. Despite the chilly weather, she wore a gauzy, earth-toned dress and brown leggings that stopped above her ankles. Bare feet (except for a silver toe ring) completed her Bohemian look.

It occurred to me this woman bore a striking resemblance to my own mother. Or at least my childhood memory of my mother.

"Who is it?" She spoke with the barest hint of a southern drawl.

Dad stood staring at me, not saying a word, just looking. It's difficult to read a virtual stranger's facial expressions, so I wasn't sure the slightly pained look on his face was surprise, shock, confusion or total animosity. Maybe a combination.

One thing I did detect was an undercurrent of cold, unadulterated fear.

Maybe this hadn't been such a great idea.

I turned to go.

"Steve, is this Skye?"

I turned back around and extended my hand. "Yes, ma'am. I'm Skye Whitmore, and this is my son, Blake."

"You don't remember me, I guess. I'm Marylou Crenshaw." She extended her hand to me.

Ah, Marylou. The woman Dad had married after Mom died. I'd met her once, at fifth-grade graduation or something, but I wouldn't have been able to pick her out of a crowd.

After shaking hands, Marylou turned to Blake. "You look like a boy who likes Rice Krispies Treats."

"Yup," Blake replied.

"Yes, ma'am," I corrected him.

"Yes, ma'am," Blake said.

Marylou smiled. "I made a batch and I could use an official taste tester to tell me if they're any good. Steve, why don't you take Skye out to the lanai? It's toasty warm out there, and I'm sure you two have a lot of catching up to do. We'll bring out some refreshments in a few."

Marylou and Blake disappeared down the hallway. Dad led me to the family room off to the left, which I couldn't help but notice was filled with lots of family pictures of him and Marylou and their two beautiful, smiling daughters. I also couldn't help but notice there wasn't a single picture of me, not even my college graduation one, and I'd graduated cum-laude. I'm sure I sent him one. Maybe I didn't. I meant to. It's the thought that counts, right?

Dad led me through a sliding door and into a sunroom that had me thinking we'd stepped into a Pier 1 showroom. Filled with dark rattan furniture and green, palm-frond-themed cushions, it was just this side of being overdone. The dark slate floor looked serviceable and easy to clean. Very comfortable and relaxing, and nary a touch of white as far as I could see. I liked it. Maybe Marylou could help me de-white my home in Gloucester.

I slipped off my leather coat and settled on a swivel rattan chair. Dad perched on the edge of an identical chair across from me. A small glass-topped table separated us.

We sat there, not speaking, each swiveling nervously in our seats. Okay, so this wasn't exactly the Hallmark reunion I had romanticized in my head. There wasn't a single hug or tear or confession of fatherly or daughterly love that had endured through the years as my child-self had always dreamed about.

Life never quite turns out as we imagine, does it?

The silence hung heavy. Gawd, how I wished I had a glass of wine right now to settle my nerves, but I figured the odds of Marylou serving a nice pinot grigio with the Rice Krispies Treats was slim to none. Not to mention the fact it was only 10:45 in the morning. A little early to start drinking, even by my standards. I cleared my throat. "So," I said, unable to disguise the nervous edge to my voice, "how've ya been?"

"Fine," he said. "I didn't know you had a son."

The accusatory edge to his voice dumped a whole heaping truckload of guilt over my head.

I cleared my throat again. "Sorry I didn't keep in better touch, but I got my own life going and you were busy with all that Navy stuff and starting your second family." 'Tis better to give than receive when it comes to guilt. I tugged at the knees of my jeans so they weren't bunching up around my hips, and then settled back in my chair. The ball was in his court.

Dad looked at the door as if he were contemplating the odds of a successful escape. That gave me an opportunity to study him. My son had my dad's eyes, skin tone and mouth shape. Hopefully he'd get some of that height, too.

Kenny, Blake's father, and I divorced shortly after our son's birth. I'd always thought Blake looked like Kenny. But, sitting here across from Dad, it hit me. Kenny was the spitting image of my father. Wow. I could have saved myself a lot of heartache had I been diagnosed with Like-Father-Like-Husband Syndrome thirteen years ago.

Dad interrupted my self-psychoanalysis when he turned to me and asked, "Why do you want to know about the house with the blue door?"

"Small-world story for you there," I said. "A friend of mine inherited the house and he showed me a picture. I have this vague feeling of something happening there that I should remember. But I don't. I was hoping you could fill the empty spaces." There, it felt good to get that off my chest.

My father got a case of the jimmy-leg, and he ran his hands through his thinning hair then scrubbed his face. "Well," he said, settling his brilliant green eyes on me, "what exactly do you remember?"

"I remember living there with Mom while you went to your ship. Honestly, I don't know how we ended up in Hutchins instead of with you."

"Your mother's mother knew the woman who owned

the house. I can't remember her name."

"Alice Fisher."

"What?"

"Alice Fisher was the name of the lady who owned the house."

"Yeah, that sounds familiar. I think your grandmother and Alice were friends or something. Anyway, you and your mom moved in with her."

"Why?"

"She had rooms to rent, and it was cheap."

"But it was a two-hour drive from the naval station."

"I was getting ready to deploy for six months, maybe longer. I was only an ensign and not making much money."

After a few beats of silence, I whispered, "It was only a matter of money?"

"Hell no, Skye." My father shifted in his seat before his nervous leg started jimmying again. "Life is never that simple. It was your damned mother, too, wanting some space to set up an artist's studio, of all the fool things. That house had an attic where your mom could work. I don't get all the questions. You were what, three-years old?"

"Four."

"Four, then. Anyway, you only lived there for about six months before, well, you know."

"Before Mom died, you mean?"

Dad's jimmy-leg got a whole lot worse. He looked at me, then at the ceiling, then at me. "You don't remember, do you?"

"Remember what?"

"That house on Periwinkle Lane is where your mother was murdered."

CHAPTER FOUR

Murdered?

That's a hard word to wrap a mind around.

My mom had been murdered.

Not just died, but had her life ended at the hands of another human being.

A memory popped into my mind. A vivid memory. The kind that completely transports you back to another time and place.

I'm dressed in my mother's favorite outfit for me, green shorts and pink shirt with flowers, and sitting at a wooden kitchen table covered in cigarette burns. It makes me feel closer to her when I wear it. I reach out to tuck my hair behind my ear and my green bow falls out, again. I pick it off my lap and place it on the table.

"How many times do I gotta tell you to get that dirty thing off my table?" Aunt Martha's raspy voice makes my skin crawl.

I give her the stink-eye. She is wearing the same ugly pink bathrobe she's worn every day since I arrived. It's covered in food stains, and it smells. She smells. The house smells. I hate it here.

She lifts a brown cigarette and tucks it between her pale lips while using both hands to fill a rusty teakettle. Once filled, she turns to the old white stove and lights the burner. The cockroaches scatter.

"Can I have something to eat, please?" I ask.

Aunt Martha takes a long drag off her cigarette and exhales smoke through her nose. With the cigarette dangling from her mouth, she shuffles across the floor, tripping over the curled edges of the dirty linoleum. She opens a cupboard, grabs a box of Fruit Loops. At another cupboard she picks up a Corelle bowl. She swings by the fridge that barely works and grabs some milk that I know from experience will be sour. She throws everything on the table in front of me. "Dinner of champions," she says. "Eat up."

I wish my momma were here to fix me my favorite hot dogs chopped up in macaroni and cheese. "When is my momma coming to get me?" I ask.

"Your momma ain't never coming to get you," she says in her raspy voice. "Your momma is dead. D-e-a-d, dead. She fell and hit her head and all her blood ran out. And your daddy's away at sea and won't be back for a long time so it's just you and me, kid." She cackles like the Wicked Witch of the West.

I start to cry.

"Mom. Mom!"

I felt a tug on my sleeve which brought me back to the here and now. Blake was standing next to me. I hugged him close, using his body to warm mine because it suddenly felt chilled. Not just chilled, but tundra cold to the bone.

"Mom," Blake said then pointed to Marylou. "She says I can call her Grandma. Is that okay?"

I put my hand over his and drew it down to his side. "It's not nice to point," I whispered to him, and then tugged him closer. I looked over at Marylou, sitting next to my dad, her hand slipped into his. They looked like a couple of teenagers on their first date.

"I'd be honored if he called me Grandma. My girls are too busy to even think about starting families right now," Marylou said.

"That would be great." I smiled at Marylou. "Thanks."

Blake wiggled out of my grip. "Here, you gotta try these Rice Krispies Treats. They're really good. Grandma put peanut butter chips in them. You should get the recipe."

"I will," I said, fairly sure I'd made them for him once and he'd hated them.

Marylou handed me a champagne flute filled with orange juice. "And you might want to try a mimosa. My specialty. You're looking a bit peaked."

I was feeling more than peaked. It was more like the lightheadedness you get when standing on the precipice of the Grand Canyon without a rail to keep you from falling down into the chasm.

A sip of the mimosa, heavy on the champagne, helped bring me back a few feet from the edge.

I sat back in my chair and listened as Marylou facilitated a conversation between Blake and Dad as they got to know each other. It gave me something to think about other than the whos/whats/wheres/whys/hows of my mother's murder. Oh, so many, many more questions that now needed answers.

Dad answered the million (give or take a few) questions Blake threw at him. Interesting to learn Dad had never killed a pirate but had chased some off the coast of Somalia. Also interesting to learn that Dad had been the kicker on his high school football team the year they'd won the state championship. I'd never known that. There was a whole lot of stuff I didn't know about my own dad. Maybe it was time to change that.

Blake, who had been standing up the entire time, sat down on the chair next to me. "Grandma says there's a park at the end of the street that has a skateboard ramp and she thinks there's an old skateboard in the garage from when her girls were skaters. It's pink, but I don't care. Can we go down and try it out?"

"I'll take him," Dad offered.

"Do you have a helmet he can wear?" I asked.

"It's purple," Marylou said.

"That's okay." Blake was halfway out the door, my father a few steps behind.

That left Marylou and me alone, sipping mimosas (round three, for anyone counting) and getting to know each other.

"Sorry to just appear on your doorstep," I said. "I hope I didn't ruin your plans for the day."

"Not at all." Marylou relaxed back into the thick cushions of her chair. "You got your father out of painting our closet, but that honey-do can wait until next weekend. I'm glad you're here. I've been pestering your father for years to find you."

"I'll take part of that blame. I could have found him, too."

A moment of tension-filled silence stretched between us.

"I'm not good company right now. Dad just told me my mother had been killed. I never knew . . ."

"How could you not know?"

"Aunt Martha told me that Mom had hit her head and died. No details." Maybe that was all my young mind could process, but you'd a thunk that sometime in the ensuing thirty years someone would have sat me down and told me the brutal truth. But then again, my thirty-four-year-old self was having trouble processing the brutal truth.

I drained what was left of my mimosa, the tangy concoction jolting my salivary glands. I smacked my lips, and then used the back of my hand to wipe them dry. "How, ah, exactly did she die?" My abdominal muscles tightened in preparation for receiving a sucker punch to the gut.

"Your father doesn't like to talk about it much, but I do know she hit her head."

"I'd heard that part. I was wondering about the murder part."

"There was some talk she was pushed. And something about a man she was having an argument with. In her bedroom."

Slowly, as if my brain was filled with maple syrup, I managed to connect the dots. Mom had been having an affair, had an argument with her lover, and he'd killed her. He'd pushed her, and she'd hit her head and died. "Who was the man?" I asked, not really sure I wanted to know the answer.

"I don't remember. It was so long ago."

"Was he ever convicted?" I hoped they'd hung him up by his *cojones* and slowly lowered him into a vat of boiling tar.

"I heard he died before there was any arrest, so he was never convicted in a court of law or anything."

"Oh." The first tear slipped out, then another. Then an entire waterfall of the blasted things.

In a heartbeat Marylou was in front of me, pulling me to my feet and wrapping me in a motherly hug. She rubbed my back as I cried and cried for the mother I had never really known. A mother who had been murdered and nobody had told me. And I cried for myself, because I didn't realize until right then how much I missed the woman who had brought me into this world.

CHAPTER FIVE

We parted company that Saturday afternoon with my promise to be in touch. Blake and I enjoyed the rest of the weekend at the beach.

I didn't ask any more questions of my father or Marylou that weekend. It's not that I didn't have a gazillion more questions than when I'd arrived, it's that I wasn't even close to being prepared to hear the answers. In fact, I wasn't sure there was enough wine in the world to help me deal with those answers.

We arrived back in Gloucester to a rare early-March snowstorm. Schools were cancelled the next day. My office was closed so I stayed home with nothing to do. I could hear the screams of the kids having fun outside. Snowball fights, sledding down the steep hill at the end of the neighborhood and making snow angels. I didn't have a single great-kid memory like that. Mine were all of Mean Old Aunt Martha who never once, as long as I'd lived with her, let me do anything fun. She always warned me I would either get hurt or get dirty, as if those were cardinal sins.

By two o'clock that afternoon I was on my second hot buttered rum and the urge to fire up the computer and do some Internet research on Mom's murder was too strong to resist. So, I gave in. Settled on my leather sofa with my snuggly Sherpa blanket tucked across my legs and my iPad in hand, I drilled into the archives of the Hutchins Daily Press. Their banner promised information as far back as 1845. I only needed to go back to June 15, 1983.

I entered the search and fourteen articles with Mom's

name popped up. The first was on June 16th that year, and the last one six weeks later.

My finger hovered on the computer's mouse with the cursor pointed at the link to the first article. Once I knew the truth there was no going back. I would have to accept it. It would probably change my perception about my entire life. With one click, my world would be forever altered.

I heard the front door slam, followed by voices of a raucous band of boys as they tumbled into the house. They came into the family room, all with rosy cheeks and icicles hanging from their hair.

"Fire," one of them said, and they all gravitated towards the fireplace where they warmed their hands, toes and backsides.

"Mom, can you make us some hot chocolate?" Blake asked.

"Please," I prompted.

"Please," they all said in unison.

"I baked some sugar cookies this morning." Don't be too impressed, they were slice-and-bake.

The boys cheered and high-fived and started roughhousing as if they were outside. "Hey, hey," I said. "Not in the house. Take your wet clothes off and put them in the laundry room and I'll run them through the dryer."

As they headed towards the small room off the kitchen, I heard Jason, the smartest kid in sixth grade, say, "Let's play poker."

"Chips only, no real money," I called after them. Jason was also a card sharp. I hoped when he grew up he'd use his intelligence for good.

The boys settled down. I fixed them their hot chocolate, going so far as to boil water on the stove instead of nuking it (just call me Martha Stewart) and plated the cookies. As soon as I felt confident the boys' thawing had begun, I retreated upstairs to my bedroom with my Sherpa blanket, iPad and yet another hot buttered rum.

The sounds of raucous laughter made me smile.

Nothing warms my heart more than the sound of kids having fun. I thought I detected the faint smell of smoke, but it wasn't unusual for a downdraft of wind to blow some of the smoke back into the house. I played a few games of FreeCell, having lost my nerve to read the articles about my mother's murder, and tried not to think about what was behind the blue door of my nightmares.

The boy's voices from downstairs became louder and the smoky smell became stronger. "Everything okay down there?" I called.

A chorus of yeahs assured me all was well.

Things grew quiet again.

The aroma turned acrider. The voices grew to shrieks. When the smoke detector chirped its warning, I rushed downstairs. The fear of fire destroying all I held dear had my heart pounding in my chest. As I ran, I pulled my cell phone from my pocket in preparation to call 9-1-1.

As I neared the family room, the smoke detector quieted. Still, I raced on, expecting the worst. I found four boys sitting around the card table near the fire, involved in a friendly game of Texas Hold 'Em.

"What's going on?" I asked, not totally buying into the angelic looks on their faces.

"Nothing," they answered in unison.

Everything looked okay. Everything smelled okay. Everything sounded okay. Except for my heart, which was still pounding like a snare drum and felt like it might jump completely out of my chest. I made a mental note to add a little more rum to my drink.

As long as I was downstairs, I decided to put the boys' wet snow clothes through a dryer cycle. When I entered the laundry room, I found a stack of my new kitchen towels, which had been white (to go with the new carpet— I know, what was I thinking, right?) only now they were soaking wet and charred almost beyond recognition.

I held Mom-Court there on the spot. "Blake, get in here right now!"

A sheepish boy joined me.

I pointed to the towels. "Well?"

The story came out that the boys, still chilled from being outside, had shoved seven more logs onto the fire, which then crackled, popped, and rolled out onto the hearth. The tongs and poker were not designed to shove heavy, blazing logs back into an over-packed fireplace. Logs had dropped, sparks had flown, and soon they had a campfire smoldering in the middle of the family room. They used wet towels—my kitchen towels—to grab the burning logs and toss them out into the snow.

"You had to use my brand-new towels?" I asked Blake.

He shrugged. "Jason said we should use a fire extinguisher before the whole house burned down. But I told him no, because you get all pissy when I use one."

As he soon learned, I also got "all pissy" when he didn't use one.

"Do you realize you could have burned down the house?" Something inside me snapped and my voice rose to that of a crazed seagull. My arms flailed like a bird about to take flight. "You could have burned yourself. Your friends. Killed the dogs. For God's sake, you could have turned us all into crispy critters!"

"Geez," he said. "It was only a little fire. Don't you think you're overreacting a bit?"

That stopped me in my tracks. I wiped the bit of spittle from the corner of my mouth, patted my hair back into place and calmed myself down. Smoke was no longer present in the house, but the acrid smell was wafting in my mind, pulling and tugging at a memory. Something about a fire that had happened a long time ago.

I'm sitting in a small room. The ceiling slopes down almost to meet the floor, making it too small for an adult to stand in, but perfect for me. The room is all white, except for a blue rag rug in the middle and a small blue door that leads out to my mom's studio. The only furniture in the room is a child-sized table and chairs, currently hosting a teddy bear tea party.

I curl up in a little alcove by the lone window. This is my favorite place because I feel like a bird in a nest, looking down on the street from my perch high in the house. With so much sunshine it's a perfect place to look at picture books and play with my dolls.

I need to dress Barbie for her date with Ken. All of her clothes laid out in front of me. Should she wear her green dress or her purple one?

Momma is in her studio talking to someone. Momma has lots of people come up to look at her paintings. Sometimes I go and meet them and sometimes I stay in my room and play.

The voices get louder. Momma is yelling.

I'm used to Momma yelling. She and Daddy yell a lot when they are together. I don't like yelling, so I do what I always do and start to sing my favorite song.

"Down by the bay, where the watermelons grow, back to my home, I dare not go . . ."

I stop. It's very quiet now. Much better. Barbie decides to wear her shimmery green dress for her date. I help her dress fix her hair.

Now what shoes to wear?

I stop and listen. It's quiet in Momma's room. The only noise is the sound of sirens. They get really loud. So loud I can't hear myself sing.

I stand up and go look out the window. Fire trucks are pulling up to the curb in front of our house. I call to my mom for her to come see, but she doesn't answer. I walk over to the blue door and reach for the doorknob. Ouch! It's burning hot. I pull my hand away. It smells funny. Like when Daddy lights a fire in our fireplace. And the room is filling with smoke just like . . .

"Mom, Mom!" Blake's voice pulled me back to the present, standing in my cold laundry room. "Can I go back and play with my friends now?"

"Sure, honey." I leaned against the washing machine and replayed the wisps of the memory. Sitting there in that playroom was the last time I remember hearing my mother's voice. It had come from the other side of the little blue door as she'd yelled at someone. Had I heard the argument that had precipitated her murder? Could that be the repressed memory trying to work its way out? Or was that just the tip of the memory iceberg?

To quote my BFF, un-effing-believable.

That strong memory triggered by the smell of smoke left me feeling a bit weak in the knees. Make that a lot weak in the knees.

I crawled upstairs and curled up with my Sherpa blanket and iPad. It was still set on the page of the Hutchins, North Carolina, Daily Press. This time I clicked on the link. Time to get some answers about my mother's murder.

CHAPTER SIX

Hutchins Daily Press
June 16, 1983

WOMAN MURDERED

Our small town, known for its sweet tea and southern hospitality, has not seen a murder in over twenty years. That all changed last night when Karen Marie Hilliard Crenshaw, aged 25, was found dead in the home of Alice Lynde Fisher. Preliminary reports show that while Crenshaw suffered a head injury, she died from burns suffered when her clothing was deliberately set on fire. She was found in the attic of the house at 230 Periwinkle Place, where she was living with a family friend while her husband, Ensign Stephen G. Crenshaw, was stationed aboard a destroyer in Norfolk, Virginia. The only potential witness to the murder was their daughter, Skye Crenshaw, aged four, playing in a small alcove off of the attic. She had to be rescued by firefighters through a window but suffered no injuries. Police Chief Allen Burns said an investigation into the murder is on-going and refused further comment.

A fleeting thought: *This explains my fear of house fires.*

I didn't stop to analyze or process or even let it sink in. My finger clicked through the next thirteen links, only to be disappointed as not one single bit of new information appeared. Until the last one.

Hutchins Daily Press
August 31, 1983

SUSPECTED KILLER FOUND DEAD

Nathanial James Coffey was found dead from a gunshot wound in his home at 489 Shore Drive in Hutchins in what police are calling a suicide. Coffey had been under investigation for the murder of Karen Marie Hilliard Crenshaw, who'd died on June 15th from burns suffered when her clothing had been doused in mineral spirits and then set on fire. Crenshaw had been staying with a family friend on Periwinkle Place, which is where the murder occurred. Sources close to Coffey said Crenshaw had been last seen leaving the Fazio's Food Mart around noon the day of her death. Coffey was seen accompanying her, carrying two bags, as they headed east on Elm Street in the direction of Periwinkle Place. Those familiar with the area know that Coffey's home on Shore Drive is west of Elm Street. Coffey had been considered a person of interest in Crenshaw's death, but no formal charges had been filed.

Investigations into both deaths will continue.

Adrenaline surged through my body, making me jittery and nauseated. So many thoughts ran through my mind—mostly, the horrifying idea that I had been in a position to save my mother from her killer. Only I'd been too interested in dressing Barbie for her date with Ken. Add doses of guilt, horror, confusion and deep, dark pain from scabs ripped off wounds I didn't realize I had, and I was, in a word, a mess.

I reached for my phone and, despite trembling fingers, managed to call Libby.

"What's up, sugar?" she asked.

"I know how my mom was killed."

"I'm on my way."

Libby was the best BFF in the world. No questions asked, no mention of more pressing issues in her own life, no worries about dinner left half-cooked on the stove or that the snowy roads might be treacherous. With those seven little words, she was on her way.

I sat curled up in my blanket wishing I was a smoker because I needed something to occupy my hands and my mind. I'd smoked my last Virginia Slims the night before commencement exercises at UVA when I'd chain-smoked so many I'd made myself sick.

As I sat in my bedroom with the white carpet and bare white walls (no time to hang pictures yet) I picked at the fuzz on my Sherpa blanket and waited for the shock to wear off. It didn't. If anything, it got worse.

It seemed like a decade, but probably wasn't more than twenty minutes before I heard Libby come through the front door. I definitely owed her one. Big time.

"Hey, boys," I heard her say. "You look hungry. How about I call for a pizza?"

Judging by the cheers, they liked the idea just fine.

Libby came up the stairs, talking as she walked towards my room. "One large pepperoni and cheese." She gave my address then rattled off the credit card number, as anyone who does lots of online shopping is able to do. "There's an extra ten in it if you get it here in thirty."

Then she was there, in my room, handing me a bag of Cheetos and a pint of mint chocolate-chip ice cream. This girl had nursed me through many a break-up and knew my comfort foods of choice. I wasn't sure Cheetos and ice cream were going to get me through this one, though.

She tossed the food on my bed, walked into the bathroom and returned a few moments later with a box of Kleenex. Then from her purse she pulled a bottle of Grey Goose vodka.

"You know what my momma always told me. 'Vodka is made from potatoes. Potatoes are vegetables. Vegetables are good for you.' So, drink up."

Libby always knew how to make me laugh. Back in college, we'd been very good about drinking our "veggies," but had throttled back on the high-proofs and switched to wine as we'd matured. But today I needed a good dose of the stuff that's "good for you."

Libby uncapped the bottle and offered it over. I took a swig and knew then that, with a little help from my friend, I was going to get through this.

The tears came before the words, but eventually I shared with her what I'd read and what I remembered.

"Ah, sugar," she said before wiping the Cheetos dust off on her designer jeans then leaning in to hug me. "I don't know what to say to make you feel better. You know you were only four-years old, so if you had gone out there to try to save your momma, that man would have probably killed you, too. Then I never would have had a roommate who talked me out of marrying Scotty the Shithead and then I never would have gotten back with Mudge and had this wonderful life I have right now. So call me selfish, but I'm glad you didn't go in there to help."

That made me smile—a little—through the tears.

"And I am so sorry I ever showed you that picture of the house. I should have kept my big fat mouth shut."

"No," I said. "Believe it or not, I'm glad you did. I needed to find this out."

"If I learned anything in that intro psychology class back at UVA it's that now you need closure." She gave my back a pat then pulled away so she was looking me straight in the eyes. "How about a road trip?"

"Huh?" I said.

"I say we drive down and visit that house with the blue door. Mudge said things should pass through probate in about two weeks and he'll get the keys to the house. Maybe you seeing it will chase all those bogeymen away."

Or maybe the bogeymen would catch up to me. And then what?

CHAPTER SEVEN

Hᴜᴛᴄʜɪɴs ᴏʀ ʙᴜsᴛ.

That sign, painted by Libby, boasted tall, fluorescent letters embellished with hippie-style, flower-power artwork and would have looked fabulous tacked to the back of a VW bus. Instead, it was taped to the inside of the tinted rear window of my midnight-blue Dodge Caravan.

The minivan was packed to the gills. Blake was loaded up with books, video games and sports equipment. The pups were tucked in their crates. And now it was time to say goodbye. At least two dozen people—neighbors, friends, co-workers, and book club members—lined Poplar Lane to wave us off on our new adventure. We were decamping to Mudge's new house. It seemed the best— no, the only—way to deal with the ghosts of my past.

My return date to Gloucester was indefinite.

It had been Mudge's idea. He needed someone to sort through the crap (he'd used a stronger word) and fix up the house before selling. I wanted—make that needed—to spend time in the house that held so many hidden memories. And maybe I'd get the "closure" that Dr. Libby said I needed. Win/win. I hoped.

Over the course of the past few weeks I'd quit my job, found a renter for my home (I shuddered to think what the white carpet would look like when I returned), and done what was necessary for Blake to transfer schools. Hutchins or Bust, indeed.

Time to go. One last hug for Libby, though. That brought on the waterworks from both of us, eye-rolling from Blake, and yipping from the pups because they hated more than anything being locked in their cages in the back of a van that wasn't going anywhere.

Finally, thirty minutes beyond my planned departure, I pointed the nose of the minivan south on Route 17. We were off.

Georgette, the name I'd given to the voice on my GPS, got us from point A to point B without incident. We stopped only once because my DNA carried the Cracker-Barrel-loving gene, making it physically impossible for me to drive past one without stopping in for a Country Fried Breakfast with biscuits and sausage gravy. With a side of grits, of course. Yum!

By two o'clock that afternoon we were pulling into the driveway of 230 Periwinkle Place. I stopped and sighed. A long driveway led up to the two-hundred-year-old home. The large, three-story coastal house stood bathed in the early afternoon sun, glowing like a Thomas Kinkade painting. It was a white house with white trim (what is it with white in my life right now?) and a red tin roof. Towering magnolia trees stood sentry in the front. Peony bushes lined the sidewalk leading from the street to the house. I sensed, rather than saw, the expansive bay beyond the backyard fence. For the first time in my life, I felt like I was home. Odd, huh?

I used the key Mudge had given me to let us in to the cold, creaky and slightly musty house.

"Wow," Blake said before running off to stake one of the six bedrooms as his own.

"Wow," I said while looking at the kitchen. And that wasn't "wow" in a good way. More like "Yuck." I'd stepped into a time-warp and was back in the 1970s, complete with butcher-block countertops, red-painted cabinets, goldenrod appliances and a curling and faded linoleum floor. Hard to ignore the wallpaper border of apples and pears that I suspected was intended to tie the yellow appliances to the red cabinets. The crown jewel— and I mean that in the most facetious way possible—was a red Formica and chrome dinette set tucked under a window with a view blocked by an overgrown lilac tree. Major, with capital M, A, J, O and R, renovations would be needed before the house could be sold.

The kitchen hadn't changed since my visit in 1983. I lingered there, waiting for the memories to swallow me up. I wasn't sure what to expect. Certainly not an avalanche of recollections from the time I had lived here, but at least a tug of nostalgia, or a vague feeling, or something familiar. But what I felt was a big, fat, emotionless nothing.

Still hopeful, I wandered to the family room. This was slightly more modern, maybe redone in the early 90s when darkly painted walls had been all the rage. The burgundy color was okay (it reminded me of my favorite wine) but the wallpaper border done in a geometric pattern assaulted my sensibilities. The threadbare, overstuffed furniture might have been unsightly but it looked comfortable. A good place to curl up with a good book. And there were plenty of good books available on a built-in bookcase that commanded the entire south wall. On the opposite side of the room was a very impressive stone fireplace. The mantel was filled with an assortment of framed pictures. One in particular caught my attention. It had a prominent position, front and center, placed to draw the most notice. It wasn't the placement, but the subject that caught my eye. The picture showed me and my mom and a lady who I can only guess was Alice Fisher, sitting on the steps in front of the blue door of this house. This brought on a soupçon of familiarity. Yeah. There was hope this would work.

Before I could study the picture further, the doorbell rang. I answered it to find a group of young boys, ages six through early teens, I guessed, with baseball caps on and gloves in hand.

"Are you Mrs. Whitmore?" the tallest of the boys asked.

"Yes I am."

"My momma heard you were coming and that you have a boy. We thought he might want to go play ball with us. There's an empty lot at the end of the street. He'll hear you if you holler loud enough."

Blake called from the hallway. "I'll get my mitt." He ran out the backdoor to the van, still packed to the gills. This could take a while.

"Why don't you all come in and sit while Blake looks for his glove?" I offered.

"Um, no thanks," the spokesman for the group said.

"Are you sure?"

"No offense, ma'am, but we aren't allowed to go in this house on account of the murder. Momma says it's possessed by the devil."

I smiled. Small towns, gotta love 'em. "That was almost thirty years ago. Certainly, the devil has moved on to other places."

"No, ma'am. It was last June when Ms. Alice was killed. Right up there." He lifted his baseball glove to point at the attic window. "Some guy pushed her down the stairs and she hit her head and died."

A cold, creepy feeling spread over me.

Two murders in the same house. Both involving head injuries. Both in June. Un-effing believable.

CHAPTER EIGHT

The backdoor slammed and Blake raced past me out the front door, his worn-out but much-loved catcher's mitt in hand. He'd been too fast for me to grab his hat and turn it around so the bill was facing forward. Backwards baseball caps are a pet peeve of mine.

"Hey, where are the pups?" I called after him.

"Sleeping," Blake called over his shoulder and he and the kids raced down the sidewalk.

Considering my canine companions had howled and yipped the entire journey from Gloucester to Hutchins, it was no surprise they'd crashed. That gave me time to explore the house a bit more without them trailing behind or getting into trouble, as they had a penchant for doing.

I shut the heavy oak door and leaned against it while I sorted through my thoughts. I hadn't asked Libby or Mudge how Alice Fisher had died. Why should I? The woman had been eighty-six-years-old and lived in a small town where violent crime was virtually non-existent.

I pulled my cell phone out of my pocket and dialed Libby. It went to voice mail. "Hey, I found out that Mudge's aunt was murdered. Can you believe that? Kind of a creepy coincidence, huh? Anyway, just wanted to let you know we made it here safely and I'm about to start my evaluation of what all needs to be done. It's gonna be a long list, 'cuz this house is from the Brady Bunch era. Hugs to Mudge for me. Miss ya." With one tap of my thumb, the call disconnected.

Ready to resume my tour of the house, I pushed

myself off the door. Before I took one step, the doorbell rang again. I cocked my head so I could see through the etching on the glass. Expecting more boys, I found instead a short, plump, elderly lady bearing a covered casserole dish. Never one to turn away a guest bearing food, I swung the heavy oak door open. "Hello."

"Skye Marie Crenshaw, as I live and breathe!"

I hadn't been called Skye Crenshaw since I'd married Blake's father thirteen years ago.

"I hope you like chicken and rice casserole. It's got lots of mushrooms and almonds in a heavy cream sauce. Comfort food at its best." The casserole-carrying woman stepped into the house and headed straight for the kitchen as if she owned the place. What could I do but follow?

By the time I got into the kitchen, the woman was shutting the oven door. She then fiddled with the knobs on the old stove. "You'll need to cook it for another thirty minutes. Then you can refrigerate it and then heat it up whenever you get hungry." She turned to me while slipping her navy-blue windbreaker off her shoulders. "I didn't expect you to arrive quite this early today. You kind of took me off my game as I'd intended to cook then chill this before you arrived. But here you are and here I am and now we can catch up." She slipped her jacket over the back of one of the dinette chairs then made herself at home. She patted the seat next to her. "Sit. Let's chat. I'm guessing you don't remember me."

I slid across the seat's vinyl surface and settled my arms on the red Formica table.

"Of course, you were just an itty-bitty thing when you lived here with your momma. My name is Ruby Labrecque. You called me Miss Wooby when you lived here as a child because your Rs hadn't developed yet."

A sense of familiarity wafted from the deepest recesses of my mind. I searched her face for a recollection of her. Nothing specific, but I had a vague sense of liking Miss Wooby. Then and now. Especially after getting a whiff of that casserole baking in the oven. It smelled delicious. "I can assure you my Rs are fully developed now, Mrs. Labrecque."

"Miss Ruby to you."

"Miss Ruby it is.." I smiled.

"Great. First thing I want to tell you that I suspect you don't know is that I have some of your mother's artwork hanging in my home."

Wow. It never occurred to me to ask if any of Mom's art existed. I felt like fireworks going off in my stomach. While Mom might be dead, a tiny part of her lived on through her art.

"Your mother said I was her best customer. Must have bought a half a dozen from her in the short time you lived here. I've sold all but one. It's of you hunkered down in a bed of periwinkle, sniffing the blossoms. It's a big piece of work, maybe five by eight, hanging over my mantel. You've got visitation rights whenever you want to come see it. My home is next door." She waggled her thumb towards the east.

Tears flowed freely. I didn't even try to stop them. There was a whole lotta emotion at the thought of seeing that painting. "I would like that. Very much. How soon can we arrange it?" I swiped the moisture off my cheek.

"I've got Bingo tonight and probably won't be back until late so how's about tomorrow, say around ten?"

"That's wonderful." Although wonderful didn't begin to describe it.

"What say we have a little celebratory toast to welcome you back to the 'hood?"

I jumped out of my chair. "Excuse me, I wasn't thinking. I should offer you something to drink. There's still a bottle of Diet Coke in my cooler out in the car. Let me go grab it."

"Sit, sit, sit." Miss Ruby waved me back into my chair then reached her hand into her coat pocket. "Have beverages, will travel." She pulled out two bottles of Mike's Hard Lemonade and put them on the table. Then she shoved a hand down the front of her sweater and fished out a shark-shaped bottle opener hanging from a chain around her neck.

Miss Ruby and I were kindred spirits.

She uncapped one of the bottles and handed it to me. "Welcome home."

Home. There was that word again. "Thank you." We clinked bottles then bottoms-upped. Yowza, that was sweet. But smooth. Mmm mmm good!

"I'll be honest with you," I said after my tongue was over the shock. "I don't remember you and nothing about this house is familiar, although it's apparent that not much has changed since the summer of eighty-three."

Miss Ruby tapped her temple with her finger a few times. "Probably a bit of repression going on in that noggin of yours. Plus, you were very young. What brought you back after all these years?"

"Twist of fate. My best friend's husband inherited this house."

"You know little Mudge?"

I laughed. "He's not so little any more. Mudge is six-foot-five-inches tall and tips the scales at over two-hundred pounds. He was a linebacker for the Cavaliers when Libby, that's his wife, first met him. Libby's my best friend back home."

"Which is where?"

"Gloucester, Virginia."

"That's where Mudge's family is from."

I nodded.

"Little Mudge moved in with Alice that summer after your mother's death. He wormed his way into all our hearts. He was the most curious little boy I've ever met."

"You'll be happy to know he hasn't changed."

Miss Ruby laughed. In a thoughtful voice she said, "Those few weeks that summer, after the tragedy, Mudge was medicine for us all. Still, we're all kind of surprised she left everything to him, considering he was only here that one summer then not so much as a postcard or birthday greeting in the thirty years since. You'd think she would have left everything to the local food shelter where she'd volunteered, or to a neighbor who'd driven her to the grocery store, hair appointments and church for the last five years with nary a complaint or request to chip in on the gas."

The expression on Miss Ruby's face led me to believe she had been the snubbed neighbor.

Miss Ruby continued, "But no, she left it all to Little Mudge. Although other than this house and what's inside, there isn't a whole lot to be had. Couple of antiques, but I'm guessing most of her stuff will end up in a trash bin."

"How long have you lived on Periwinkle Place?"

"Over fifty years. Alice was my best friend. A good woman, although having to deal with her husband's death and your mother's murder so close together took its toll. She was never quite the same fun gal after that."

"How ironic that she ended up being killed in this house, too."

Ruby choked on her hard lemonade. Using the sleeve of her red sweater she wiped off the table. "Sorry about that. Alice? Killed? Now what fool told you that?"

"One of the neighborhood boys."

"Probably Felicity Hancock's boy, Sonny. Is he a tall drink of water?"

"Yes, ma'am."

"Yup, that's Sonny. His momma, Felicity, is a trouble maker. And slightly crazy in the head, if you'll indulge this old lady a non-professional psychiatric opinion. The truth is, Alice had a bit of the vertigo and was falling down all the time. Twice, at least that I know of, in the week before she died. But the rumor mill has been running in overdrive since they learned Nate Coffey had been in the house when it happened."

Nate Coffey? Isn't that the name of the man who killed my mom and then committed suicide?

"You know the name Nate Coffey?" Ruby asked.

I voiced the question that had popped into my mind.

"Nate is Nathanial senior's son. He's probably your

age, maybe a few years older. Despite living in the shadows of his father being accused of murdering your mother, he grew up to be a nice young man. He's an attorney in Raleigh. Came up that weekend to talk to Alice about the day your mother was murdered. They were in the attic trying to go through some of her stuff that was still up there when Alice lost her balance and toppled down the steps, hitting her head on the way down."

"So, he didn't push her?"

"Of all the stupid things." Miss Ruby slammed her bottle down on the table with enough force to rattle the salt and pepper shakers. "Of course he didn't. That Nate's a nice boy. All he wants to do is clear his father's name after all these years."

"What makes him think his father was innocent?"

"He read the police file and claims there was a loose thread that hadn't been investigated."

I gave her my best are-you-goofed-on-skunkweed look. "How is anyone going to follow up on something that happened thirty years ago? People move away or die, and time has a nasty habit of changing memories. They are no longer reliable."

"When a woman burns to her death in the house next door, you don't forget it. Ever. Every detail of that day is branded on my brain." Miss Ruby took a swig of her lemonade before taking a trip down memory lane. "And here's something the police didn't follow up on, even though I told them. While I didn't see a person, there had been a strange car parked at the curb that day. It was gone before the fire started so the police chief dismissed it as not integral to the case. And he said he didn't need any more proof of Nathanial Coffey's guilt once he put that gun to his head, pulled the trigger and blew his brains all over his garage."

Okay, I could have done without that visual.

But the idea of a strange parked car had merit. And, of course, begged the question, if Nathanial Coffey hadn't killed my mother, then who had?

CHAPTER NINE

The doorbell rang again. In all my time in Gloucester, I never had more than a few doorbell rings a month. Here was my third ding-dong within thirty minutes of my arrival in Hutchins.

As the sound faded, Ruby jumped out of her seat and grabbed her windbreaker with a speed and alacrity that belied her age and size. While slipping one arm in the sleeve, she chugged the rest of the bottle of hard lemonade. "Oh, Lordy, that'll be Felicity Hancock. She'll be bringing you some cookies as an excuse to find out your story so she can be the first to spread the gossip. That girl needs a crash course in social etiquette. It's best if I keep my distance from her because she doesn't more than open her mouth before I want to slap her silly."

"That bad?"

Miss Ruby tucked the empty Mike's Lemonade bottle in her coat pocket and headed for the back door. "Worse. Be careful you don't say anything you don't want the entire town to know before sundown. And also, don't eat the cookies. She's a vegan so no butter or sugar or eggs in her baked goods. You might as well eat a rock."

With that warning, Ruby slipped out the kitchen door into the back yard, and took with her possible answers to some of the new questions I had about my mother's murder. Like, what do you suppose the odds are of tracking down a car that was parked at the curb thirty years ago? I'd say slim to none. But it was better than what I had before.

The doorbell rang again.

Not entirely thrilled at the prospect of meeting the neighborhood gossip, I didn't race to answer it. I can be passive/aggressive that way.

The visitor rang the bell two more times and knocked once. Loudly.

Eventually I opened the door to find a young girl who if not of legal-drinking age was pretty close. She wore a backwards baseball cap, flannel shirt with the sleeves ripped off, jeans with holes in the knees and checkered Vans. In one hand she held a brown grocery bag by its twine handles. Since the boy who had come to get Blake was probably around twelve, I was pretty sure this person was not his mother, the famed Felicity Hancock. "Hi, I'm Skye Whitmore," I said. "And you are?"

"The delivery girl for Fazio's Food Mart." She stood holding the bag in my direction.

"What's this?" I asked, accepting the bag. It was heavier than it looked.

"There's a note in there." She stood, her hand still held out, her foot tapping impatiently.

Her surly manner did not deserve a tip, but I fished out two bills from my pocket and handed them to her. I didn't want it getting known around town as a poor tipper. Not my first hour in town, anyway.

The delivery girl took the money and without so much as a "Thanks," turned and ran back to her battered grey Hyundai Accent parked at the curb.

I shut the door, hefted the bag onto my hip, and carried it back to the kitchen where I unpacked it. Two bags of Cheetos, three half-gallons of mint chocolate chip ice cream and two bottles of my favorite pinot noir. Taped to one of the bottles was a small card that had "Get Well Soon" crossed out and a hand-printed message in the space below. It wasn't Libby's handwriting, but it was certainly her sentiments. "Since I'm farther than across town from you now, thought I'd better stock your pantry for any and all emotional emergencies. This should tide you over until I can drive the four hours to be with you. Miss you already.

Love U lots, Libby."

That Libby. Is she the best BFF ever or what?

I stowed the ice cream in the freezer, which seemed to be working fine. Mudge had made sure all the utilities were turned on and the house habitable before my arrival.

With the Cheetos and wine tucked in a cupboard in case of emergency and Miss Ruby's aromatic casserole cooling on the counter, I set off to explore the house. With Miss Ruby's hint that some of mom's stuff remained in the attic, I felt hopeful that the process of closure would soon begin.

The house was a rambler, even bigger inside than it looked from the street. I took a quick lap of the first floor. Most of the decorations were forgettable, but the baby grand piano in the frilly living room and the crystal chandelier in the gaudy dining room might be worth looking up on an antiques website.

Upstairs I found six bedrooms and one full bath, all decorated in degrees of pink, varying from princess to dusty rose. *Aye-yi-yi.* What I wouldn't give for a plain white room right now!

Blake had staked a front bedroom for his own. It wasn't the largest, but it was the least pink of all of them. Banshee and Bella-Boo were curled up on a pale-pink chenille bedspread that had been thrown onto the floor in what I guessed was Blake's attempt to de-pink the room. Banshee opened his eye and peered at me, and then rolled over and went back to sleep. They seemed to be making themselves at home.

For myself I chose a sunny bedroom with lots of windows at the back of the house, which offered sweeping views of the bay. If I were to write a poem about this room it would be titled "Ode to a Cabbage-Rose Room." When I say the room was decorated, I really mean over-decorated, with pink roses on not only the bedspread, but the wallpaper and drapes and even decoupaged on the lampshades. I didn't remember which room had been mine when I'd stayed there with Mom, but I think it might have been this one. Sans cabbage roses, that is. I'm sure I would still be having nightmares about them.

That left one final frontier to be explored. The attic. I drew a few fortifying breaths, and then ascended the narrow and creaky steps, they type scary movies used to foreshadow extreme danger. Was I a bit creeped out? Not just yes, but *hell, yes*! But this is what I'd come here to do.

About halfway up, the steps took a dog-leg to the left. As I rounded the turn, I was able to see the attic's layout. A room off to the right was a bedroom with a bare mattress on a Jenny Lind bed and one dresser. Off to the left was my mom's art studio. I headed that way first. There were two shelves filled with her tools of the trade: rusty soup cans with dried-out brushes sticking out at all angles; tubes of paint; Styrofoam cups; and tons of general crap. On the easel was a painting in progress, a tangible connection to my mother. I ran my fingers over the scene of a lazy river in fall. That simple gesture seemed to evoke an intangible sense of my mother's spirit. I don't want to go all metaphysical here, but I definitely felt my mother's presence. It was comforting and calming and tear-inducing. I used the back of my hand to swipe away the moisture on my cheeks.

Five boxes labeled "Karen's Things" were tucked behind the easel. They looked promising, but before I got the first one opened, a small door tucked along the wall caught my eye. The door to my playroom.

I walked over and tried to open it. It was stuck. With a little effort and the aid of a screwdriver used as a lever, I managed to get it open. A musty odor wafted out, but didn't deter me. I got down on my knees and crawled into the room.

It's a rare occasion when a grown woman is transported back in time to her childhood. Most rooms grow with the child before being turned into craft rooms or exercise rooms once the baby bird is pushed out of the nest. This tiny playroom appeared undisturbed since the day I had been sent off to Mean Old Aunt Martha's. Same white walls and multi-colored braided rug and table set for a teddy bear tea party.

My emotions ran high right now. Off the chart. I felt closure coming on. Thank goodness Libby had encouraged me to take this journey.

As I turned to crawl back out, I spotted an old cardboard box marked in black Sharpie words, *Skye's Stuff*. Again, that feeling of standing on the edge of the Grand Canyon washed over me. Too many emotions made me dizzy. But I couldn't *not* open it, could I?

Inside I found a few dolls and doll clothes, none of which looked familiar. I picked up a tattered pink blanket, and decades-old muscle memory lifted my thumb to my mouth as I stroked the soft satin border with the other. Blake had done the same thing with his blankie. I tossed it aside and dug deeper into the box through layers of toddler clothes, which I assumed I'd outgrown and were tucked away for baby number two. When I reached the bottom of the box, my fingers brushed across something hard. Like a book. I pulled out a white diary. They vinyl was cracked and the pages yellowed. I'd been too young to write, of course, so it couldn't have been my journal. Curious, I opened it. It cracked in protest, the slight noise echoing off the rafters. Inside were many pages of elegant flowing script. The ink had faded, but the words were, for the most part, readable. I started on page one.

January 1, 1983. New year, new life, new possibilities, so much excitement for what lies ahead. I'm finally going to focus on my painting. But there's also the dread of Steve leaving for his first overseas deployment. Six months apart from him. It's the Navy way, I know. I can do it. It will be easier for me because I have Skye. He'll be all alone. If all goes as planned, we'll be together as a family for Christmas. I so hope this year flies by.

Look at me, wishing my life away again. Mom always scolded me about doing that, but I've been doing it since I was a teenager, always wanting to be older and for time to pass faster, especially in Algebra class!

Anyway, happy New Year to me. To us. To everyone. I have a feeling it's going to be a year of many of changes.

Wow. I could hear my mom's voice while I read that. A strong memory hit me, of being held tightly in Mom's lap while she read softly into my ear the words of *Goodnight, Moon.* Kind of freaky. But in a good way. This was the closest I'd been to feeling a connection to the house and my mother and the events of thirty years ago. This is why I needed to come and stay in this house.

I flipped through the book. There were pages and pages of entries, going all the way through to June 15, 1983. I would need a glass—or more like a case—of wine to drink while reading through this.

Holding the journal tightly, I left the playroom and made my way to the part of the attic that served as a bedroom. The one with the Jenny Lind bed, which I thought would be as good a place as any to curl up and start reading. Before I made it across the room, I noticed scorch marks on the floor.

This is where Mom had been knocked down, doused with highly flammable mineral spirits and then set on fire. Some repair work had been done in the eaves, but telltale signs and scents of a fire remained. On this floor, in this spot, was where Mom had drawn her last breath.

My chest tightened and it became hard to breathe. I wasn't sure what a panic attack felt like, but I feared I was fixin' to learn. I needed to get out of this space. I never should have come up here. I wasn't ready to face this. Not yet. Not alone.

I scrambled back towards the stairs, still clutching the journal. My legs were shaking, my insides felt quivery, and there was a good chance I was going to toss my cookies. I had to get out of this attic. Now.

As I reached the top step, the doorbell rang, startling me. My foot went slightly sideways and caught the lip of the top step as it went over the edge. Down I went, tumbling ass-over-tea kettle, screaming my fool head off the entire time.

I had one thought as I landed at the bottom. *Isn't this exactly how Alice Fisher had died?*

CHAPTER TEN

I wasn't dead. At least not yet. But I sure did hurt. Everywhere, from my head to my toes. I felt a warm dampness seeping through my shirt and suspected it was blood. I had a vague memory of a rusty old hook scraping flesh off my arm on the way down.

"Hello?" a male voice called from downstairs.

I tried to answer, "Up here," but what I had intended to be a yell came out more of a whisper. The pain ripping through my rib cage let me know I shouldn't have whispered that loudly.

"Hello? Hello?" The man kept calling. I listened as his footsteps moved around the first floor, slowly at first, then more frantic.

Mustering up all the strength in me, I yelled, "Help!" It might have been little more than a squeak, and it hurt like a son-of-a-bitch, but he heard me.

"I'm coming," he called. Footsteps pounded up the stairs, and in a heartbeat he was next to me.

A warm hand reached out and grasped mine.

I opened my eyes enough to see a man, about a nine on the one-to-ten scale (I knew I couldn't be too injured if I was still able to rate a guy on the hunk-scale), dark haired, well-dressed, and about my age. Reaching into the pocket of his leather jacket, he extracted a cell phone. With one thumb he began pressing the screen. "Hang on, I'll get an ambulance."

I gave his hand a squeeze. He squeezed back.

"I have a woman here at two-three-oh Periwinkle

Place in Hutchins who needs an ambulance. Yes, she's conscious but weak. I'll ask." He turned to me. "What happened?"

"Fell." I used a shaky index finger to point towards the attic steps.

"She fell down a flight of steps. There's blood. A lot of it. Very awkward position. She can move her fingers, but I don't know about her toes. Okay. Hurry."

He dropped his phone and looked down at me. "The ambulance will be here soon. They said not to move you, in case your neck is broken. I need to cover you with a blanket so you don't go into shock. Be right back." He left.

I closed my eyes. And then nothing.

* * * * * *

When I opened my eyes again, it felt like I was six inches away from bright headlights on a Mack truck. The pain was intense, so I closed them. That simple action had taken a lot of effort. I needed more sleep. Before I could drift off, I heard a voice.

"Skye," Libby said.

Libby was here? Where was I?

I lifted one eyelid again, just far enough to see Libby's tearstained face right next to mine.

"You're gonna be okay, sugar. I promise."

"Blake," I whispered, and then licked my parched lips with my sandpaper tongue.

"He's with Miss Ruby. She's quite a firecracker, isn't she? She said she'd bring Blake over as soon as you were awake. I can call her right now, if you want."

"Wait," I whispered again. "How do I look?"

"Like you was rode hard and put away wet, that's for sure."

I smiled. Libby had always said that about our UVA dormmates when on Sunday mornings they'd make the walk-of-shame home after they'd been out partying a little too hard on Saturday nights.

"Am I crippled?" There, I'd voiced my worst fear. The one sparked by the words the man had said about me possibly having a broken neck.

"What? Crippled? Not my Skye. No sir. You cracked a few ribs, broke your nose, which means your gonna have a bad case of raccoon-eyes in a few days, but I've got some heavy-duty concealer that will cover that right up. Your arm got tore up a bit, but after those stitches come out, you won't have but an itty-bitty scar. Only we're going to have to come up with a better story than you falling down some stupid ol' steps. Something sexy, like a hang-gliding accident off the cliffs in Costa Rica in order to escape from some bad guys wanting to sell you as a sex slave." She squeezed my hand.

I smiled again, if only in my head. It was too much effort to move the muscles in my face.

Libby patted my good arm. "Other than that, you're fine, sugar. Just fine."

Funny, I sure as hell didn't feel fine.

"Did you see these lovely flowers here?"

I moved my eyeballs until I could see the table that supported a magnificent display of at least three-dozen yellow rosebuds on the verge of blooming. "Who?" I asked.

Libby plucked a small envelope from the middle, opened it and read, "That was quite a tumble you took. Hope you feel better soon. Nate Coffey.' Then there's a phone number from some area code I don't recognize." She waved the card in the air. "So, you're in Hutchins maybe one hour and already you've got a beau? Better start talking, sister. I want all the details about this Nate Coffey fellow."

A nurse came in before I had the opportunity to tell Libby that I knew Nate Coffey only by name as the son of the man who killed my mother and who was interested in clearing his father's name in my mother's murder.

The nurse, who was old enough to be my grandmother, shooed Libby out the door. "I'm glad to see you awake," she said to me. "How do you feel?" She grabbed my wrist and took my pulse.

"Like hell."

"To be expected. But you'll feel right as rain in a week or so. By the way, I have a message for you from your fiancé."

"My what?"

"The man who brought you in. Good looking guy."

"Leather jacket?" I asked.

"Yeah, and a nice one at that. Don't tell me he's not your fiancé."

I shook my head. *Owwww.*

The nurse lifted a plastic cup towards my mouth and pointed a bendy straw towards my lips. "Well, you must be pretty special to him. He brought you those beautiful flowers over there, and I can tell you that's more than a hundred bucks he dropped on blooms from the florist shop in the lobby."

My brain might still have been foggy but I was able to figure out that Nate Coffey was the man who'd found me and called the ambulance. I took a few sips of lukewarm water while I tried to process the information. When the effort to drink outweighed my thirst, I turned my head away from the straw. "What was his message?" I asked.

"That he has some journal of yours and to call him when you want it back."

Nate Coffey had Mom's journal. The one with all her deepest darkest thoughts. The one that connected me to her the way nothing else in this world could do. The one that might help prove his father's innocence. But what would Nate Coffey do with it if, instead, it proved his father's guilt?

CHAPTER ELEVEN

I spent one night in the hospital with Libby fussing over my every waking and sleeping minute. Her fussing included contraband Cheetos, wine, and double-stuff Oreos. Amazing what that girl can tuck into her Coach purse.

Upon my discharge from the medical center, I returned to Alice's house where Libby continued fussing. Blake did, too. Well, as much fussing as can be expected from a twelve-year-old boy. His efforts warmed the cockles of my heart, though. Banshee and Bella-Boo did their part to make me feel better by cuddling up with me. A girl could get used to all this pampering.

While I'd been lying in my hospital bed, Blake had moved in with Miss Ruby, who'd served him real home-cooked meals. He couldn't stop talking about the chicken and dumplings or the macaroni and cheese that didn't come out of a box. But despite my lack of culinary talent, he seemed glad to have me home.

Funny how I used that word "home" in reference to Alice Fisher's house. Hmm. That might bear some thinking on when I was in more of a thinking mood.

Feeling marginally better two days later, I called Nate Coffey and scheduled a meeting. He'd read the journal and had information for me. He was due any minute.

Libby had done amazing things with my make-up so I didn't look like card-carrying member of the walking dead. I had on my best purple velour warm-up suit, not because it matched the circles under my eyes but because it's better to feel good than to look good when one's ribs were healing. Libby, on the other hand, was decked out in a designer turquoise sweater set and black slacks. Her look was completed with coordinated sea-glass jewelry. A little over-the-top for the occasion of me facing yet more painful truths about my mother's life. And her death. Was I nervous? Not just yes, but *hell, yes!*

Waiting in the formal living room that had all the fussiness but none of the elegance of a Downton Abbey drawing room, I perched on a threadbare damask chair. From my position near the front window, I watched a sleek black Range Rover pull up to the curb in front of the house. Those things had a sticker price at about the same as my first house, over $70,000.

A man wearing a leather jacket and blue Dockers got out of the vehicle and headed up the front walk. He carried a bouquet of lilies (my favorites) in one hand and Mom's journal in the other. Nate Coffey had arrived. I pulled away from the window so he didn't catch me ogling him.

Libby met him at the door and showed him into the living room.

"Hi," he said, with a smile that went all the way up to his baby blues. He handed me the bouquet of flowers. "How're you feeling?"

"Better," I answered, pulling the lilies to my nose and inhaling deeply of their softly sweet fragrance. "Thank you. We haven't been formally introduced. I'm Skye Whitmore, by the way."

"Guess you don't remember, but we go way back. We were sandbox buddies. Our mothers took us to McCutcheon Park every afternoon when you lived here."

"Miss Ruby says I probably blocked a lot of that time out of my mind."

"I wouldn't blame you. I do remember you, though. I had a sand-box crush on you." He smiled.

I blushed.

Libby did the happy dance behind Nate's back. She'd have us marching down the aisle before dinner time.

I looked at her and said, "Libby, could you please put

these flowers in water? And then give us a bit of privacy."

"Sure thing, but holler if he gets fresh or anything."
She winked at me as she took the lilies then headed off to
the kitchen.

Turning to Nate I said, "Please, have a seat." I looked
forward to a little small talk with this easy-on-the-eyes guy.

He slipped his jacket off and laid it on a chair. Settling
into the seat right next to me, he leaned close and, holding
Mom's journal in both hands, said, "This is what Miss Alice
and I were looking for the day she fell. Where did you find
it?"

So much for small talk.

I leaned back in my chair, trying to find a
comfortable—or at least a less painful—position. "I didn't
so much find it as it found me. It was in a box with my
name on it."

"Do you remember anything about that day in June?"

"Bits and pieces are starting to come back," I said.
"Since Libby showed me the picture of the house, I've had
a sense of something happening here, but I'm not clear
what."

"You were in the room next to where your mom was,
ah . . ."

"Was knocked down then set on fire, yes. I do
remember hearing an argument between her and another
person right before that, but I have no idea who it was.
Why your interest in this now, after all these years?"

"My mother's deathbed confession last year. She
shared with me the truth of that summer and told me that
Dad had killed himself because of the shame brought on
the family over his suspected affair with your mother.
Mom says the rumor-mongers had him convicted of your
mother's death without benefit of a trial. He couldn't bear
it."

"You didn't know until then that your father
committed suicide?"

"I knew it, but Mom had led me to believe it had been
because of financial reasons, although I didn't learn of that

until I was in high school. Dad had been out of work for a
few months, but still kept current on a life insurance policy.
He was faced with the choice of paying on that or putting
food on the table. Problem solved with a bullet." Nate
cleared his throat. "After he died, we moved down to
Raleigh to live with mom's sister. The insurance policy left
enough money to get us through the next few years until
she'd earned her degree and found a job. That part of it
was all true, of course. But there was more to the story."

"Why didn't she ever pursue the matter herself?"

"She was afraid of the truth. Even though she believed
in his innocence and his fidelity, she wasn't one-hundred
percent convinced that my daddy hadn't killed your
momma. She liked to think he hadn't, but didn't think she
could bear the truth if he had. It's important to me to find
out what really happened."

"Are you prepared for the truth?"

His blue eyes locked on mine. "Yes. Are you?"

Like I hadn't asked myself that question a gazillion
times over the past few weeks. But this time I had a
different answer. "Yes."

Nate leaned back and crossed his ankle over his knee.
He cradled Mom's journal in his hands. "After my mom
died, I came to Hutchins and started asking questions.
Nobody I spoke to ever suspected an affair, and good luck
getting away with something like that in a small southern
town. Also interesting, I couldn't find any solid proof that
he'd even gone into the house that day, let alone killed your
mother. According to the police report, there weren't any
of his fingerprints anywhere. Way I figure it, somebody else
killed your mother. Alice Fisher remembered seeing your
mother writing in a journal and thought maybe there would
be some information in there. We tried to find it. Turned
this house inside out, but nothing. And then she fell, and I
went back to Raleigh thinking I'd never learn the truth. But
when Miss Ruby called and said you were coming to town,
I thought maybe you might remember something so I
rushed right up here."

"I'm sorry I don't have anything to tell you. But your timing was impeccable. Thanks for coming to my rescue, by the way."

"And thank you for finding your mother's journal. It supports the theory that somebody other than my father killed your mother."

A noise by the door between the living room and dining room drew both of our attention. "Libby, why don't you come in and pull up a chair so you don't hurt yourself trying to bend your ear around that corner?" I said.

"Thank you," Libby stepped across the threshold. She didn't look the least bit embarrassed at having been caught eavesdropping. She pulled a brocade side chair to our circle, rested her elbows on her knees, and then leaned into the conversation. "You were saying?"

"Ah, yes." Nate held the journal up in the air and looked at me. "I've read every word of what's in here at least a dozen times. Most of these pages are filled with how you and your mother spent your days, she painting and you hosting teddy-bear tea parties in your playroom, but it also includes quite a few passages where she professes her deep love and devotion for your father. According to this, your father was in love with another woman back in Norfolk. He'd asked for a divorce, but she wouldn't give him one on account of your mom was a devout Catholic."

"You're a Catholic," Libby interjected. "Un-effing-believable!"

I admit I was surprised, considering the extent of my religious training was hearing Mean Old Aunt Martha use God's name whenever she damned something, which was a lot.

Nate waved the journal in the air again. "There is something here that might point the finger of guilt in another direction."

"What is it?" Libby asked.

"I'll read it." He thumbed through the journal, stopping about the midway point. He slid his finger down the center, pressing it open. "Here we go." He cleared his throat. "Dated June fourteenth, nineteen eighty-three. That would have been the day before her death. It says, 'Steve is adamant about a divorce. But I won't give it to him. We had a real knock-down drag-out over the phone this morning and I'm really upset. When the conversation was over, I reminded him of our vows. ' 'Til death do us part, dear. He said, 'That can be arranged.' "

Nobody moved for the longest time.

Nate was hinting that maybe my dad had killed my mom.

I cleared my throat. "Nate, let me ask you a question. Did your mother ever tell you your father's side of the story about that day? I mean, he had to have an alibi or something."

"What my dad told my mom and the police and anyone and everyone else who would listen was that on that day he'd been out for a jog and had run into your mother, walking home from a trip into town. She was carrying two heavy bags of groceries and a large container of mineral spirits she needed to clean her paint brushes. Dad offered to help her and walked her home. Dad told my mother that when they'd turned the corner from Market onto Periwinkle, Karen stopped in her tracks. Dad said she seemed reluctant. Or maybe the word was frightened. Either way, seeing a car parked in front of this house spooked your mom. She grabbed the bags from Dad and said, 'I'll take them from here,' then rushed off, not even offering a thank you. Dad continued on his run which took him all the way down Shore Drive and back. That western edge was sparsely populated back then and nobody could provide Dad an alibi."

Like a movie, the scene played out in my mind. Then something Miss Ruby had said clicked in. "You know, Miss Ruby said something about seeing an unfamiliar car parked in front of the house on the day Mom was killed. Maybe she remembers some details about it."

Nate stood and started pacing the room, running his fingers through his hair, then swiping at his five o'clock shadow. "I read something in the police report about an unusual car parked on the street that day. It'd been crossed out. I asked why, and they said it didn't have any bearing on the case. But what if it did? I need to talk to Miss Ruby. Where does she live?"

"Next door." I wiggled my thumb in the direction of Miss Ruby's house.

"Be right back," he called over his shoulder. And then he was gone.

"What do you think?" Libby asked.

"About being Catholic?" I asked, still gazing out the window at Nate as he hurdled the privet fence between the two houses.

"No, about your dad being the one who killed your mom."

I looked at Libby who looked about as serious as I've ever seen her look. And that included the time she was about to go in front of the University of Virginia Judicial Committee for an underage drinking violation. She'd been *this close* to being expelled, and if that happened, she'd have been cut off from her daddy's money source, leading her, she feared, to a life of flipping burgers. Yeah, she'd been serious that day.

And she looked even more serious now.

That's when the gravity of her question hit me. I blew out a big puff of pent-up breath before speaking. "My mom died when somebody set her ablaze. Does that sound like something you'd do to someone who was the mother of your daughter, a woman you had loved at some point in your life?" I shook my head. "But I do think that whoever killed Mom was driving that unidentified car. I don't know if anything can be done about it thirty years after the fact, though."

Libby leaned forward and took my hands in hers. Hers felt warm. I realized mine were as cold as icebergs.

"Forget about the car," she said. "Think about the final thing your dad said to your mom. Her death can be arranged. I know you don't want to believe it, but why else would your father ship you, his only daughter, off to Mean Old Aunt Martha unless he had a super guilty conscience? It makes sense, if you ask me."

Holy crap. Dad killing Mom was a really hard concept to wrap my head around. Really hard. Starting-to-freak-me-out hard.

But a little voice in the back of my mind said it did make sense. My dad killed my mom, and then did his best never to lay eyes on me again. I would have been a constant reminder of the horrible thing he'd done.

"Cheetos or ice cream?" Libby asked.

"Cheetos," I answered.

She ran off to get a bag.

Have you ever tripped and fallen on a sidewalk, smacking your hands against the cement, at which point they start tingling painfully? That's how my whole body was feeling right now, as if every nerve ending had smacked against cement. The implication that my father might have killed my mother had even my brain tingly numb.

I stood and made a slow lap around the formal living room. Shelves tucked behind the piano at the far end of the room drew my attention. I hadn't given a second glance to them on my quick tour of the house when I'd first arrived. Studying the vast collection of Hummel figurines gave my mind a diversion. Eventually my gaze scanned the top shelf that also held snapshots tucked in gold gilded frames. Wait. *What is that one?*

I reached for one tucked slightly behind the others and pulled it out for closer inspection.

Okay, wrecking ball to the stomach moment. A family picture. My family. On Periwinkle Place right in front of Alice Fisher's house. Dad was leaning on the hood of a Ford Pinto hatchback, one the color of a school bus, while Mom was nested between his spread legs. They had their arms around each other and were gazing into each other's eyes. The camera caught me, mid-twirl with my pink dress flaring out around me, near them. The image of family bliss.

What in the hell had happened? They went from happy family to one killing the other in a few short months?

"Here you go, sugar."

Libby's voice startled me. I fumbled the frame but managed to secure it before it smashed on the hardwood floor.

Libby stood in front of me, holding a tray with not only Cheetos poured into a large cranberry-red Tupperware bowl, but also three tumblers of gin and tonics, complete with healthy wedges of lime.

"Come on. Let's sit."

We went back to the seating area and I reclaimed my spot on the damask chair. She held out the tray for me to grab a drink. I did. She noticed my hand shake as I reached for the G&T but she had the good sense not to say anything.

After putting the tray on the table, she grabbed a glass for herself and held it up for a toast. "Here's to those who wish us well, and those who don't can go to hell!" Libby smiled, but I couldn't summon any mirth for the toast that had started many a great evening back in our hard-drinking days. Nonetheless, we clinked glasses.

I took a sip—okay a gulp—of the G&T. It didn't help as much as I'd hoped. I pulled up the memory of sitting in the attic playroom and hearing the fight between Mom and another person right before she died. I tried to make the other voice sound like Dad's, but it didn't mesh with the memory. Maybe I didn't want to acknowledge the fact, but something in my gut told me it hadn't been Dad. If only I had some proof, one way or the other.

The front door slammed and Nate rushed in. "Miss Ruby says the car parked at the curb the day your mom was killed was a Pinto. The color of a pumpkin. With Virginia plates."

I looked at the picture in my hands, of Dad leaning on the hood of an orange-yellow Pinto.

Okay, so what more proof did I need?

CHAPTER TWELVE

After taking a cellphone shot of my newly discovered family photo (no way was I willing to part with it!), Nate took it, along with Mom's journal and the information about the Pinto hatchback, to the police.

He called from the road as he traveled back down to Raleigh. "They've officially pulled the investigation out of the cold-case file and are sending someone down to Florida to question your father. By the way, he asked that you not say anything if you should talk to him. They don't want him tipped off. They consider him a flight-risk."

The dad I had reconnected with was now a flight risk and a suspect in my mother's murder. Talk about a cyclone of mixed emotions.

A few moments after I hung up with Nate, Libby got a phone call that Mudge was suffering an appendicitis attack and was on his way to the hospital. She packed her bags and raced off to Gloucester faster than you could say "Happy hour!"

Blake took over the role of nurse that evening and showed compassion I didn't know he had. There was hope for that boy yet.

I had a restless night, what with the physical pain from my injuries and the mental anguish stemming from truths I'd had to face that day. Morning came as I dozed off.

Blake woke me up. "Mom. I'm leaving for school, now."

I peeked at the clock. Yikes. "Breakfast?" I asked.

"Some of the peanut-butter cookies Miss Ruby

dropped off last night."

Another bad-momma demerit for me, although probably not much worse than Peanut Butter Cap'n Crunch cereal. "Did you pack a lunch?"

"I'll buy today. It's pizza."

"Balance it with a salad."

"Whatever."

I reached up and brushed a curl off his forehead "What about Banshee and Bella-boo?"

"Miss Ruby came by a few minutes ago and took them for the day. And she said she'd check on you later." He was quiet for a moment. "Do you want me to stay home with you?"

Like I said, there's hope for that boy yet. "No, honey. You need to go to school. I'll be fine. I'll lay around and take it easy."

"Are you sure?"

"I'm sure. But as soon as school is over, I want you to come right home, okay?"

Home. There's that word again.

I blew him a kiss as he left the room then settled back down in my bed and dozed. I woke up an hour later hungrier than a bear after hibernation, so I hauled myself out of bed and down to the kitchen for sustenance. This morning, that sustenance came in the form of mint-chocolate-chip ice cream.

Today, the healing powers of Breyer's did nothing to take my mind off my worries. *What if Dad is innocent? No, the evidence is too strong against him. But his car was in front of the house the last time Mom was seen alive. Maybe it wasn't been his car? I'm sure he wasn't the only guy in the world driving a school-bus-yellow pinto. Or maybe Miss Ruby had her memory wires crossed and she'd seen that car on a different day. It had been thirty years ago . . .*

I needed to do something or go crazy. While I didn't feel up to physical tasks related to cleaning out Alice's house, I could start a list. Okay, make that some lists. Many lists of the many things that needed to be done to get this house ready for sale.

I got as comfortable as I could on the old sofa. and, with a glass of sweet tea and notebook in hand, set to work. Before I could even title the page "The list of lists that need to be made," the doorbell rang. Getting off the sofa was a painful process, but I put on a happy face before swinging open the heavy oak door.

Holy crap. Marylou stood on the stoop. Talk about the *last* person in the world I wanted to see. I mean, her husband was about to be arrested for murder, thanks to evidence I'd found. I knew the warrant was being processed, but I wasn't allowed to say anything. An actress I was not. But I was gonna have to channel my inner Jessica Chastain and pretend I didn't know anything. It took all I had in me to keep my happy face on.

"Hi, Skye," Marylou said as she stepped into the foyer. "Steve talked to Blake last night and he told us you'd suffered a terrible fall, so being the good step-mother that I am, I hopped on a plane and headed north." She reached out and wrapped me in a big hug.

"Ouch," I said as I pulled apart from her. "Sorry. The ribs still hurt. But I'm doing okay. Please come in."

"Nice house."

I looked at her and we both laughed. Thankfully, she didn't seem to detect mine had a nervous-titter quality. This acting gig was hard. "It has good bones, as they say. Can I offer you something to drink?"

We went into the kitchen. I prepared coffee and plated some lemon pound cake that one of the neighbors had dropped off. Between the welcome-to-the-neighborhood and get-well-soon food offerings, I wouldn't have to cook for a month.

I joined Marylou at the red Formica table. She was trailing her finger around the frame that held my Happy Family picture. I'd been carrying it around like a security blanket since I'd found it yesterday. It comforted me the way nothing else ever had, or probably ever would.

Marylou reached out and laid her hand on my arm. "Skye, I'm so sorry your mother died."

"It was a long time ago, but thanks."

"Your father was devastated."

Of course he was, I thought. *He killed her.*

But you'll be in a bucket full of trouble if you tip Marylou off to what you know. "You knew my dad back then?"

"He never told you?"

Puzzle pieces clicked together. "Were you the other woman? The reason dad wanted to divorce mom?"

"Where did you hear that?"

"I found Mom's journal. She mentioned another woman, but not by name."

"A journal?" Marylou took a bite of cake. "Wow, what a treasure for you. What kind of stuff does it say?"

If I said too much, Marylou could warn Dad and he could grab his passport and jump on the next plane to Bolivia, or whichever South American country doesn't extradite. Best to evade that question completely. Well, not so much evade but lie my butt off, the mere thought of which set butterflies flitting in my stomach. I may be a real estate agent, but I'm a *Truth, the whole truth, and nothing but the truth* kind.

I cleared my throat, buying time to compose my response. "I haven't finished reading it all yet, but so far it's about what we did during the day, me playing while she painted. She sounded very happy, but mentioned that my father wanted a divorce because there was another woman. So that woman was you?"

Marylou shifted in her seat and then took a sip of coffee. With her elbows on the table, she cradled the mug in both hands. Eventually she answered my question. "We'd met at a club in Norfolk. I was in the Navy, too. Enlisted, so going out with your father, who was a married officer, was wrong on two fronts. But I knew the instant I met him he was the man for me. It was kismet."

I'd had kismet once, with Blake's father. But it had only lasted a few months. Dad and Marylou's had lasted thirty years. "I understand," I said.

"Really?" she asked, sounding surprised.

"Yup. When I saw you two together in your house in Florida, I could tell you two were still in love. Everyone deserves a chance at happiness." I couldn't hold back the tears any longer. All the emotions of the past days came flowing out in one big, drippy sob.

Marylou got out of her chair and hugged me. A maternal, everything's-gonna-be-all-right kind of hug. Gentle and caring. And it only hurt my ribs an itty-bitty bit.

Funny thought: this time tomorrow, I could be the one offering comfort. Oh Lord, life sure can get messy quickly, can't it?

We needed to do something. Something that didn't require too much talking, because I wasn't sure how much longer I could keep up this I-know-something-that's-going-to-turn-your-world-upside-but-can't-tell-you charade.

An idea formed that Marylou could help me get started hauling out the stuff that wasn't worth keeping. As soon as Blake got home from school, I'd send them off for ice cream or something, and then I'd drop everything and call Libby. I needed to talk this situation through. Fortunately, she'd left my crisis-food cabinet well-stocked.

Where to start? The attic seemed logical. We could start with all those dried-up paint brushes and rusty soup cans. Having Marylou there with me would be a big help on the physical, mental, emotional and spiritual fronts. As an added bonus, I would have someone with me when I went up and down the stairs.

"Hey, enough of this," I said to Marylou. "I need to keep busy, and I could use your help, if you don't mind. I need to get the attic cleared out. There isn't much up there worth saving, mostly Mom's old painting supplies. With my ribs and all, I can't carry anything down, but I can help toss things into garbage bags."

"Tell me what you need done," she said, rolling up her sleeves. "I came here to help."

Armed with trash bags, we ascended the narrow, creaky steps to the attic and got to work. Since my ribs were still painful, Marylou did all of the heavy lifting and hauling down to the trash pile growing in the garage. *Note to self: call and have a dumpster delivered ASAP so this type of purging could be done in every room.* I looked around the room, at the masses of junk, and multiply that by over 3,000 square feet of living space. *Make that two dumpsters.*

At two o'clock it was time to stop. Blake would be home soon. There was only one more corner to go in the studio, and then the alcove where I'd played as a child. We'd accomplished a lot over the last few hours. It felt good.

"I'll be right back," Marylou said as she hefted a heavy bag over her shoulder and headed downstairs.

Wanting to get a feel for what exactly was left, I crawled into the playroom. It was a nice spring day. Still a bit chilly, but the sunshine streaming through the one small window felt warm on my face. I opened the window to get a bit of fresh air in the musty space. I sat down and tried to fight off the memories of the voices I'd heard yelling at each other the day mom had been killed. Sitting here in this room it was as if they were happening right here, right now. I couldn't ignore them.

The wind blew the little blue door shut with a bang and I jumped at the sound. Suddenly the room felt too small. Or more like I felt too big. I crawled over and tried to open the door but it was stuck fast. I'd have to wait for Marylou to return to kick it open from her side.

Maneuvering myself back to the small table set for the teddy bear tea party, I arranged the tea cups and served imaginary tea the way I had when I was little. So many happy memories of this room, of this house. Okay, so there was one really bad one that I still didn't have my head wrapped around yet, but so many good ones, too. This, I realized, was home, in every sense of the word.

All the crawling around in this small room made my ribs hurt, so I laid down and stretched out in an attempt to get comfortable while waiting for Marylou to come back up and open the door. The memories of the day Mom had been killed replayed in my mind again, this time so real I could smell the smoke. I heard the voices again, arguing loudly. I tried to listen past myself singing the "Down by the Bay" song. It occurred to me the person arguing with Mom was a woman talking in a low and with a slight southern drawl. If I didn't know better, I'd say it sounded like Marylou.

Holy crap. The idea felt like a two-by-four smacking me upside the head. It had been Marylou fighting with Mom. I closed my eyes and listened again. Now that I've heard her voice and synced it with my memory, there was no doubt in my mind. She's the one who'd doused Mom with mineral spirits and set her on fire, leaving her—and me—to die!

I sat up and looked towards the door. Small tendrils of smoke seeped in around the cracks. It wasn't memory smoke, it was really smoke. The attic was on fire.

I ran to the door and pulled, but it was locked from the outside. I banged and shouted until my hands were numb.

There was no one out there to save me.

I ran to the window and looked out. Three stories up was too high for me to jump. I yelled for Marylou, then realized her rental car was gone from the curb. Of course it was. She was going to kill me the same way she had my mother. She must have realized how close I was to figuring out she'd murdered my mom.

"Help! Help!" I screamed my fool head off. My throat hurt from a combination of screaming and from the smoke. I started coughing while screaming and my screams became weaker. It occurred to me I might not make it out of this attic alive.

"Help!" I screamed again, but it was a pathetic effort, at best.

I spotted a group of boys walking down the sidewalk, pushing and shoving each other in fun. A huge dose of adrenaline kicked in and gave strength to my voice. "Fire, Fire," I called out as loud as I could. "Help! I'm trapped.

Call the fire department."

Blake looked up, hesitated only a moment then dropped his backpack and came running. Full speed.

Sonny pulled out his cell phone. I hoped he was calling 9-1-1.

The smoke was getting worse. I looked over my shoulder to make sure the flames hadn't broken through yet. Once the fire was through that door it would only be a matter of minutes before this old braid rug and dried timber walls—and me—went up in flames. I hung my head out the window in an attempt to fill my lungs with sweet, fresh, smoke-free air.

It's not true. Your life doesn't pass before your eyes when death is near. Your future does. Scenes of things you hoped to accomplish and enjoy and experience. I'd never grow old, never see Blake grow up, and never ever hold my grandbabies.

Stop thinking like that I told myself. *Look for a way to live!*

I noticed Miss Ruby had joined the group of school boys. She wrung her hands and crossed herself repeatedly.

What's that sound? Sirens. In the distance! Maybe the fire department would get here in time to save me!

My hopes lifted and I strained my eyes to see them come around the bend. But nothing. The seconds ticked away as the sounds on the other side of the door got louder. The flames would be upon me soon. It was only a matter of moments.

"Mom, Mom," I heard Blake's voice on the other side of the door. "Don't worry. The fire's almost out."

Blake My son. My savior.

"It's too hot for me to get over to the door, but the flames are out."

After that, everything seemed to be happening at once. The fire trucks arrived and within minutes had a ladder up to my window. A fireman was there, giving me oxygen and then helping me out the window to safety.

Blake was waiting for me at the bottom of the ladder. I wrapped him in a great big hug while tears streamed down my face.

"This young man saved your life," a fireman told me. "He used a fire extinguisher and had most of the fire out before we got here."

Blake hugged me. "I know you get all pissy when I use one, but I didn't have time to get wet towels."

"I promise not to get pissy this time." I pulled him close. "But I might get all kissy! Come here, you wonderful son, you."

CHAPTER THIRTEEN

It was a Disney-movie kind of day as friends and family gathered in the backyard. Blake, Libby, Mudge, Miss Ruby, Nate, and I crowded around a picnic table and enjoyed an early summer picnic of ham biscuits, potato salad, and dill pickles. Homemade strawberry ice cream waited in the freezer for a treat after we finished the croquet challenge Nate had devised. Banshee and Bella-Boo snoozed in the shade of a stately Bay Oak tree. Birds were chirping, leaves were rustling, and the sun was shining I felt happy and relaxed and settled. After searching my entire life, I'd finally found my home.

"The house is looking good, Skye," Libby said.

"Still a lot of work to be done." The fire hadn't caused too much damage, but the house still needed some major renovations before selling. I planned to speak to Mudge about buying it for myself. It was more than the memories of the past, it seemed to be my future, as well.

"Can I go play ball now?" Blake asked. "The team needs me."

"Go on," I said. He loved living in Hutchins as much as—maybe more than—I did.

My phone buzzed in my pocket. Checking Caller ID, I saw it was my father. We hadn't spoken since Marylou's arrest. It was time. "Excuse me everyone. I need to take this. It's my dad."

Libby reached out and gave my hand a squeeze as I slipped away from the picnic table.

I walked to the back of the yard where a tangle of

honeysuckle all but obscured the chain-link fence dividing my property from the marshland that led to the bay.

"Hi, Dad."

"Hello, Skye. How are you and Blake doing?"

"Fine. And you?"

"It's been pretty rough, but I'll get through it. I am so thankful you're okay. I don't know where to begin . . ."

I waited for the beginnings of a statement or a confession or an apology or something, but none came. After a deep breath, I asked, "Did Marylou confess to killing mom yet?"

"No, but the prosecutor thinks the similarities between what she did to you and how your mom died are going to be enough proof. It'll be up to the jury, though."

I had faith in the justice system. "I'm sorry, Dad. That's gotta be rough for you."

"We've got a good lawyer, of course."

"Of course." I looked at the house that I now called home. There were some awful memories there, but some good ones, too. "Hey, I found a picture of our family. You're sitting on the hood of a school-bus orange Pinto hatchback, holding Mom in your arms."

"Yeah, I saw that picture. It's the evidence that will be introduced against Marylou, since that was her car that someone spotted in front of the house that day."

"Her car? So, you were already together with her? But you looked so very much in love with Mom."

"Despite what you think you saw in that picture, Skye, things hadn't been good for your mom and me for a really long time. I did love your mom, but we wanted different things out of life. She'd never supported my decision to join the Navy in the first place. Your mom wanted us to live a bohemian life, with her painting and us traveling 'wherever the light was best,' she always said. But how was I supposed to provide for my family moving from one temporary job to another?" Dad paused. "Karen compared us to a dandelion. I was the root and she was the pappi. You know, the white fluffy tufts that float on the breeze.

Nature designed them to be separated at some point."

I spotted a fluffy-white dandelion at my feet and bent over to pick it up. Mom had loved dandelions. She'd hold one out for both of us to blow on, like blowing the candles out on a birthday cake. We'd make a wish as the seeds dispersed into the wind. I added this to my growing repertoire of happy mom memories.

Dad continued talking. "I loved the Navy, enjoyed being at sea. It's what I wanted to do with my life. Your mother moved to Hutchins, hoping I'd follow. But I didn't. I got lonely. And, well, things happened."

"I understand you loving Marylou, but I never understood why you abandoned me."

"Abandoned you? I was always only a phone call away, and you know I bought you everything you ever wanted."

"I don't mean financially, Dad. You abandoned me emotionally."

A moment of silence hung between us while I twisted the dandelion between my fingers.

Finally, Dad spoke. "At first, Martha asked that I stop calling because you were so upset after you hung up. Then the few times I did get through to you when you were older, you made it clear you wanted nothing to do with me. You said you were happier without me."

It's true. I had said as much to my dad. But it had been the pain and loneliness speaking. I hadn't meant it.

"I only wanted you to be happy, Skye, so as much as it hurt me, I left you be."

I didn't know how to respond to that. Not right now, anyway. We obviously had a lot of talking yet to do, and we needed to do it face to face, not over the phone.

"Skye, I know I never showed it and I certainly never said it, but I do love you."

I love you too, Dad. I thought it, but I didn't feel ready to say it out loud.

"I gotta go." There was a catch in his voice.

I closed my eyes and blew the fluff off the dandelion. *I wish strength for both me and my dad as Marylou's murder trial progressed.*

He disconnected the call. Reluctantly, I did too.

I walked back to the picnic table where my friends were eating, drinking and being merry. They got serious upon my return.

"Is everything okay?" Libby asked.

"They've lawyered up," I said. "Marylou hasn't confessed, so it'll be up to the prosecutor to convince the jury. I suppose there's a chance she'll walk."

"Un-effing-believable," Libby said.

"Here's hoping that she never sees life on this side of the prison fence again," Nate said as he raised his glass in the air.

I lifted my glass of pinot grigio and clinked glasses with everyone then took a sip.

A gentle breeze blew, rustling the leaves of a maple tree in the back corner of the yard. I pointed to it and said, "I'd like to build a memorial garden under that tree. I'll fill in the entire area with periwinkle vines, like Mom dreamed about."

"That's a great idea, Skye." Libby slipped her arm around my shoulders and gave me a squeeze. She had been with me every step of this emotional healing process. I was going to hate not living close to her, but she'd only be four hours away, and she always stocked my shelves with enough wine, Cheetos and ice cream to get me through a crisis until she could drive down and be with me. But I had a feeling there wouldn't be too many more crises. Now that I had all the answers as to what lurked behind the blue door, the worst was behind me, and the future seemed bright here in Hutchins, North Carolina.

"It amazes me Marylou got away with murder for thirty years," Mudge said.

"And she might have gone thirty more if Nate hadn't decided to clear his father's name." I reached over and slipped my hand into his. "I'm so sorry you had to go your whole life thinking you were the son of a murderer."

"I always knew in my heart my dad hadn't killed your

mom. I'm only sorry it took me so long to prove his innocence." He squeezed my hand and smiled.

An ice cream truck made its way down Periwinkle Lane, its tinny tune brought a smile to my face. "Down by the Bay."

Nate started singing along. "Did you ever see a dog, chasing a hog, down by the bay?"

"That's not one of the verses," Libby said. She was an expert on children's songs, with her background in pre-school education.

Nate smiled. "Our mothers made up all sorts of silly verses to that song. Didn't they, Skye?"

Little snippets of memories bombarded me: young Nate and me swinging side by side as our mothers pushed us higher and higher; young Nate and me splashing in the shallow water of the Albemarle Sound; young Nate and me sitting Indian style during story time at the library. And yes, young Nate and me and our mothers singing silly "Down by the Bay" verses as we sat under a tree enjoying a picnic of peanut butter and jelly sandwiches. That was a nice memory. I suspected there were many more nice memories to be uncovered.

I was at peace with my decision to make the move here permanently. The circle of happiness would be complete if Nate were here, too. But that's not a topic I was ready to discuss with him yet.

Miss Ruby offered her goblet for a toast. "I've reached that age where my brain went from 'You probably shouldn't say that' to 'What the hell, let's see what happens.' So, here goes." She paused, cleared her throat, and then lifted her chin. She looked Nate square in the eyes. "You gonna keep on living the city-slicker way? Or are you gonna move back here to Hudgins, where you belong?"

Nate looked at me and smiled. "I'm moving back," he said. "Since I'm no longer the son of a murderer, I can hold my head up high."

I smiled back at him as my heart did a little flutter, the

way a heart does when there is love and hope of a forever-and-ever-amen joy hanging in the air.

A peek at Libby across the table from me revealed she was happy for me. Her eyes twinkled with tears as she raised her glass of wine in my direction. After all, she wasn't losing a best friend, she was gaining someone to take care of me between her visits to my new home, down by the bay.

THE END

SEAS THE DAY

"Seas the Day" finds best friends Connie Baker and Monica Lyn Hunter searching for evidence of dishonest business dealings. Instead they discover a dead body. Things go from bad to worse when they decide to dispose of the body in order to frame someone else. Everything spirals out of control when they become suspects in the murder.

SEAS THE DAY

I've never seen a dead body up close and personal, let alone one chopped up like a fryer chicken and stuffed into two Hefty Cinch Saks. It's not a pretty sight, and it's accompanied by an even more ghastly smell. I fought down the vomit burning my tonsils and stumbled out of the garage as fast as my linguine legs could carry me.

"Well?" Monica Lyn Hunter, my best friend since preschool, asked.

"That's a real dead body all right." I gave into gravity and melted down onto the driveway. The heat from the blacktop warmed by a late August sun seeped through my cotton capris but did little to soothe the post-horrific shock rattling my extremities.

"Not a mannequin leftover from Halloween or something?" The tone in Monica Lyn's voice bordered on a whiney panic.

"Mannequins don't smell. Nor ooze blood. Go call the police."

"No police." Monica Lyn twisted her long dark hair into a bun on the back of her head, then released it, allowing it to cascade down over her shoulders. She did it again. And again. And again.

A nervous sort of chuckle gurgled from my solar plexus. "Yes, police. Now."

Silence. "We can't."

"Why not?"

"They'll think J.J. had something to do with it."

The J.J. to whom she referred was Joseph Jackson

Hunter III, Monica Lyn's soon-to-be-ex-husband. It was his garbage can we'd roped to the tow hitch on her F-150 and rolled the six blocks to her parent's house, where she was temporarily living until the Family Court judge decided who got custody of her and J.J.'s McMansion on the hill.

The plan had been to paw through J.J.'s discards in hopes of finding incriminating evidence regarding his illegal business dealings, which Monica Lyn had long suspected but never proved. This would then be hung over J.J.'s head in order to procure a more Monica Lyn-friendly divorce settlement. I didn't consider it blackmail—that's such an ugly word—but more like marital justice.

"A dead body in his trashcan trumps an embezzlement scheme any day," I explained to her.

"J.J. couldn't have done it. He passes out at the sight of blood."

"Then how do you explain the dead body?"

"I can't. Yet."

"I'm calling the police." No sooner had I fished my iPhone from my pocket than Monica Lyn snatched it from my hands and tossed over the fence into Mrs. Gardener's backyard. For the record, the neighbor's name wasn't really Mrs. Gardener. My small, seaside hometown is big on nicknames and had bestowed the Gardener moniker upon her decades ago when she'd created a beautiful English garden in the center of town square. That was the sum total of her gardening efforts, and long before I came around, so I honestly don't know her real name.

"Reality check," Monica Lyn said to me. "That hacked up body is in my garage, with our fingerprints on the trashcan handle. And look, you've got blood on your hands."

I looked down, and sure enough, my French tips were splattered with red goo. I swiped my hand against the grass, but the evidence remained, pulsating like a Jackson Pollock version of The Telltale Heart. Not only did I look guilty, I was beginning to feel guilty.

Monica Lyn started pacing like a high-strung thoroughbred before being loaded into the starting gate at the race track. "Nobody is going to believe us when we say we found the trashcan at J.J.'s house. They'll think we killed him. Her. It. No, calling the police is Out. Of. The. Question."

When Monica Lyn resorted to a speaking style that punctuated after every word, there was no room for rational counterarguments.

I drew a deep breath of late-summer honeysuckle air and let it out in a Lamaze-style breathing technique that had brought me little relief when I'd given birth to my only son twenty-one years ago. It didn't help much in this situation, either. "What exactly do you have in mind?"

She stopped pacing, punched her fists to her hips and said, "We can haul it up the street to Kitty Kline's house."

Kitty Kline was our sworn archenemy. The reason: she'd sprouted breasts in fifth grade and they'd still been growing when we'd graduated from Rocky Shoals High School. The boys had all loved her. The girls had all hated her. And after all this time, apparently still did. "You haven't gotten over that boyfriend stealing incident?" I joked. That had happened in eighth grade. Twice.

"Not a boyfriend. A husband."

"You mean Kitty Kline's the scrawny blonde crack 'ho . . ." My voice trailed off when a look of complete disgust washed over Monica Lyn's face. I wished I could take back the mental image I'd planted in both of our heads. Monica Lyn had yet to find the strength to share all the sordid details of discovering J.J.'s cheating ways, but I knew it involved her early return from a city council meeting to find J.J. and the aforementioned SBCH (scrawny blonde crack 'ho) enjoying a game of Strip Billiards. A dead body delivered to Kitty Kline's doorstep seemed a good first step on the road to healing. Plus, it would keep me from having to answer a lot of questions from the police.

I took another swipe of my nails against the grass. "I'll

need a glass of wine first."

"I'll need a bottle," Monica Lyn said.

* * * * * *

Monica Lyn and I had shared our first bottles of Boone's Farm Strawberry Hill on the night of her 14th birthday. That had been twenty-eight years, three months and six days ago. I still had a Jimmy Buffett lyric tattooed on my backside as a souvenir.

In honor of my first visit to my hometown after a twenty-five-year absence, Monica Lyn had purchased a case of the beverage that more closely resembled cough syrup than cabernet. We each grabbed a bottle and, armed with a bucket of ice, headed for the back patio to figure out a plan. With her parents decamped to their mountain cabin for the summer (it was cooler there, and wasn't plagued by tourists), we had the house to ourselves. In hindsight, it would have saved us a lot of grief if Mr. and Mrs. O'Neill had been around to talk us out of our simple (yet stupid) plan.

"Seas the day," she offered up in our time-honored toast. We clinked glasses, then settled back to enjoy—and that's an exaggeration, it was more like endure—the sweet wine.

As soon as it was nice and dark and we were good and drunk, we donned matching pairs of yellow Playtex Living Gloves and hauled the trash can up the center of Cottage Street to Kitty Kline's house. Our fumbling fingers dropped the trashcan more times than I cared to count, which required us to chase it as it rolled down the hill towards Sagucci Bay, which got us to giggling so much on at least three occasions we had to slip behind Mr. Magoo's (another nickname for a man who scraped his car on a daily basis) lilac bush to relieve ourselves. Unbeknownst to either of us, we'd left a trail of blood leading from Kitty's curb straight back to Monica Lyn's garage.

Once we reached our destination, we parked the trash

can in the small patch of weeds that constituted a front yard. It felt good to be rid of that body. "Time-a call-la police," I sang while performing a sloppy Running Man dance move.

"Sssshhhh," Monica Lyn shushed me. "Don't wake Mizzizzizz Kravitz."

Mrs. Kravitz (real name: Peterson) was the nosy body of Sagucci. Monica Lyn and I had bestowed upon her the nickname based on a character in the TV show "Bewitched" after she caught us sneaking out of Monica Lyn's bedroom during the wee hours on a school night. The old biddy had squealed on us to our parents. Her generally accepted nickname was Mrs. Muffin—she baked the best blueberry muffins this side of the Mississippi— and lived two doors south of Kitty. Not a thing happened on this street without Mrs. Muffin/Kravitz/Peterson knowing about it. She had been older than dirt when I'd lived on the north end a quarter century ago. Hard to believe she was still alive, let alone still poking her proboscis into everyone else's business. I held a finger to my lips and repeated in a loud whisper, "Call-la police."

"Okey dokey." Monica Lyn bobbed and weaved her way up the steps to Kitty's front door.

"Whatareyadoin'?" I whispered more loudly than I should have, given the circumstances.

"Needda phone."

"Wherezhyur cell?"

"I dunno. 'Sides, cops 'ud trace it back ta me."

I smiled and nodded at Monica Lyn's criminal brilliance. "Jus' don't wake Kitty," I cautioned.

"Car's gone," Monica Lyn said, her Living Glove-clad hands twisting the door knob, to no avail. "Prob'ly out screwin' someone else's husband." She stopped twisting and, with exaggerated movements, crossed her arms under her breasts. "Now, if'n you were an SBCH, where wouldja hidda key?"

We stood side by side, under the porch light, and surveyed the possibilities. "Flower pot," I said, because that was the only thing sitting on the rust-stained cement porch. .

Sure enough, tucked under a terra cotta pot filled with water-starved petunias we found a silver key that granted us access to Kitty's home. I waited in the front room and counted the Chinese takeout containers (my comfort food of choice, also) on the coffee table while Monica Lyn made the 9-1-1 call.

Once the proper authorities had been notified, we skedaddled back down Cottage Street. Ensconced once again in Monica Lyn's parent's fenced-in patio, we collapsed on the chaise lounges and then proceeded to toast our success with a few more bottles of Boone's Farm. "Seas the day!"

There were a lot of toasts. Who'd a thunk that dragging a dead body around would be such thirsty work?

* * * * * *

There are hangovers, and then there are HANGOVERS. I currently suffered from the latter, and right now wished I was in a simple pine box buried six feet under the ground.

Instead, I sat in an echo chamber labeled Police Interrogation Room Number Three, baking under lights that had to be 2,000 megawatts brighter than the sun.

"I'll repeat my question," Detective Dirk Rasmussen said. "How did you and Ms. Hunter come to be in Ms. Kline's house?"

I forced myself to open my eyes and peeked at the man lounging in a metal chair. He was light-skinned, dark-haired, and built like a cuddly teddy bear. But the expression on his face more closely resembled a lion sizing up his dinner. I had a sinking feeling I was to be the main course.

"What makes you think we were in Ms. Kline's house?" I asked. My recollections of the previous night were vague. Okay, more like non-existent. That Strawberry Hill wine had a tremendous amnesiatic effect.

"Because Mrs. Peterson reports seeing you and Ms. Hunter entering Ms. Kline's house at two fifty-eight this morning. That's one minute before a phone call was placed from that location, informing us of a dead body in the front yard."

"Maybe Ms. Kline made the phone call herself. Did you ever think of that?"

"I find that highly unlikely, considering it was her body in the trashcan."

I laid my head down on the cold metal table, closed my eyes, and connected the dots of the previous day's escapades. The dead body in the trash can we found at J.J.'s house was that of his playmate of the month, Kitty Kline. And it had been pilfered by his soon-to-be-ex-wife, a very jealous Monica Lyn, and delivered to her front yard by Monica Lyn and her childhood friend—me. It seemed a logical conclusion that one of the three of us had killed Kitty. The only thing I knew for sure was that it wasn't me. "I want a lawyer," I told the detective.

He nodded and left the room.

* * * * * *

Since it was determined that Kitty Kline had been dead for a couple of days and I had an airtight alibi working at my job at a cotton merchant more than 1,000 miles away in Memphis, Tennessee, I was off the hook for murder. Charges for accessory after the fact, breaking and entering, and urinating in public were still pending, but the attorney I found in the Yellow Pages had me sprung on my own recognizances by suppertime. And just like in a bad movie, I'd been warned not to leave town.

Monica Lyn wasn't so lucky. With means, motive, opportunity, not to mention the trail of blood down Cottage Street, she was a slam dunk for the prosecution. But the judge took into account her twelve-year stint as a city council woman, nine years as Girl Scout Troop 83 leader, six years as PTA President, and current fundraising chair for the local no-kill animal shelter, and deemed her a low-flight risk. Bail was set at an amount easily covered via a cash advance on her VISA.

A smart woman would let the police take it from there. A really smart woman would hire a private investigator to help things along. And then there's Monica Lyn. She decided to take things into her own hands.

"I need your help," she said the next afternoon. I'd just returned from picking up my favorite lunch from my favorite local restaurant—spring rolls from Maya Moons Chinese Restaurant—which I placed on the table. I had lived on Maya Moon's spring rolls back in high school. Literally. A fad diet I'd read about in a teen magazine had suggested the best way to lose weight was pick one favorite food and eat it exclusively for one month and the pounds would melt away. (The theory being, I guess, is that you get tired of the food and don't eat as much of it.) I had picked spring rolls, because I loved them, and I figured they were filled with vegetables, therefore, a healthy option. But I hadn't counted the carbs in the flaky wrapper or the fat grams from deep frying the egg roll-like food. Nor had I tired of eating them. Thus, I ended up gaining weight—and picking up the nickname Spring Roll—by the end of the month.

I hadn't had any near as good since I'd left town. My mouth watered at the aroma, but my stomach did a crazy flip-flop at the look on Monica Lyn's face. I wasn't sure what kind of "help" she needed, but this didn't bode well.

Monica Lyn was already unwrapping the first spring roll from its waxed paper bag. My choice, as I saw it, was either to abandon my all-time favorite food that I hadn't tasted in over a quarter of a century and run screaming for the hills, or I could sit down at the table and share the delectable spring rolls with her and then run screaming for the hills. At least Plan B would allow me to run on a full stomach.

I slid my backside along the mahogany bench seat the way I had at least a million times in my youth. So may memories. Especially the one where I'd been an accomplice when Monica Lyn had used her brother's wood burning set to engrave ML+JJ=4EVER in the corner. I let my fingers trace the letters and contemplated how sometimes mathematical equations don't always prove out.

"Whadaya have in mind?" I asked, my voice revealing the hesitation I felt. Monica Lyn had changed since being released from what she now referred to as her two-day vacation in cell block number thirteen. Her eyes, once dancing with mischief and merriment, were now iced-over with misery and fear. I had a bad feeling about this.

She took a long draw on her Earl Gray tea then thumped her mug down on the table. "When the police questioned J.J. about the trashcan we found in his garage, he made up a crazy-ass story about how I was not taking the divorce well and had cooked up this scheme to pin the murder rap on him, when really I had been the one who'd killed Kitty. So, time for us to flip the tables back around and we're going to do whatever is necessary to make sure J.J. is accused of Kitty Kline's murder. That way he gets to spend a few days rotting in jail. Then we'll do our civic duty and find the real killer, since the cops don't seem too keen on examining the evidence. It's a win-win, don't you agree?"

"We? As in you and me?"

Monica Lyn nodded.

"No way. Not me. I'm washing my hands of this whole thing. I already regret helping you steal the trash can in the first place. 'What could go wrong?' you'd said. Turns out, everything could go wrong. And then your stupid plan of planting the evidence at Kitty's house almost got me ten years to life. No way. Not me. Find yourself another partner in crime." I scooched towards the end of the bench, dragging a spring roll through the sweet dipping sauce as I slid past.

But Monica Lyn put her size ten bunny slipper on the edge of the bench and stopped me from leaving.

"Are we or are we not sandbox sisters?" she asked.

I stared right back into her baby blues. "We are. BFFs since age two."

"Did I or did I not beg my family to take you in last semester of senior year so you didn't have to move to Reykjavik, Iceland, with your mother when she married that crazy sailor?"

"You did." A marriage that had lasted 179 days, at which point Mom became a global vagabond. I'd seen her twice since.

"Did I or did I not stop, drop and roll you when your veil caught on fire at your wedding reception?"

"You won money from America's Funniest Home Videos with it."

She wagged her pointer finger at me in a tick-tock motion. "But that hadn't been my motivation. I did it to keep you from flaming up like a Roman candle and having that beautiful face of yours disfigured for life. Risking my own beautiful face in the process, I might add."

I let my gaze drop to my fingernails, which I'd scrubbed to bleeding nubbins in an attempt to remove every last molecule of Kitty Kline's blood.

"And who was it that rushed to your side to hold your hand while Lucas drew his last breath?" she asked.

"You." My mother had been MIA somewhere in Thailand while my husband battled pancreatic cancer.

"And did I or did I not lend you my last dime to help cover the funeral expenses?"

This could go on forever. "Okay, I get the point," I said.

Monica Lyn settled back on her stool. "Have I ever once asked for anything in return?"

"No." And she hadn't. Ever. Not one single time since our sandbox days.

"I'm calling in all my BFF chits right now."

"Now?" I re-tallied the friendship account. I owed her. Big time.

"Now. Go get dressed in something you don't mind getting dirty." She lowered her slipper to the floor.

I could leave. I could get up and walk out of this house and trot down to Gillian's Wharf Road where I could hail a pedicab and have him take me to the nearest bus station where I could board a Greyhound and ride off into the sunset.

Or I could stay and help my best friend exact revenge on her dirt bag of a husband who had tried to convince the police this kind, gentle soul was capable of murder.

I knew what she would do if I asked her.

"We're going back to the house . . ." Monica Lyn said.

By house I knew instinctively she was referring to the McMansion where she and J.J. had lived for seventeen years and raised two kids. But ever since she'd returned early from her meeting to find J.J. and Kitty in a compromising position, it had ceased to be her "home" and was now merely "the house."

"We'll wait for him to get home from work. Then we'll get him so schnockered that when we tell the police he confessed to the murder, he won't remember if he did or not. Ready?"

"I guess."

* * * * * *

Calling Doctor Morgan. Doctor Morgan. You're needed, stat." J.J. waved his empty tumbler in the air in a sloppy drunk way.

As bartender for the evening's festivities, I concocted another pitcher of Dr. Pepper and Captain Morgan's Spiced Rum (aka a Dr. Morgan), heavy on the rum, and poured another round. So far, the plan seemed to be working well.

We'd spent the last few hours sitting poolside, sipping the rum beverage and reliving the good old days of The Four Musketeers, which had consisted of me, Monica Lyn, J.J., and his younger-by-three-minutes twin brother, Scott. Last I heard Scott was serving a twenty-year sentence for running a methamphetamine lab in Cincinnati. And I'd come *this close* to marrying him.

"Seas the day!" We all raised our glasses then drank. "This is better than my fourteenth birthday party," Monica Lyn said, wiping tears of laughter from her eyes. We'd sure had some great times as kids.

I poured another round. "Promise me you won't make me get another tattoo to commemorate the event."

Monica Lyn laughed so hard she fell out of her chair. J.J., ever the gentleman, helped her back up. I poured us all another round of Dr. Morgans.

"You have a tattoo?" J.J. asked. "Do tell."

"Not just any tattoo. A misspelled one," Monica Lyn said. "Only we didn't realize it until the next morning when I looked at her ass." Monica Lyn spoke through chortles and snorts. "Instead of 'Wastin' away again in Margaritaville,' it says 'Bastin' away.' " She laughed so hard she fell out of her chair. Again.

"I don't believe it," J.J. said.

I got up and tugged the waistband of my capris low enough so he could see the misspelled lyric, a forever reminder of when we'd been young and foolish. And drunk.

Now we were middle-aged and foolish. And drunk.

"Your turn," I said to J.J. once we'd all stopped laughing and got ourselves off the ground and back into our chairs.

"Yeah," Monica Lyn said. "True confessions time. Tell us one of your deepest darkest secrets."

He swirled his drink in his hand, the ice cubes clinking softly against the glass. "Have I ever told you about the night Kitty Kline was hacked to pieces?"

I felt like I'd been hit by lightning, the way my arm hairs snapped to attention at not only J.J.'s words, but the foreboding tone of his voice. I held my breath, waiting, afraid of what he'd say, but also strangely curious to hear the macabre tale.

The sun had set hours before, leaving J.J.'s face cast in wavering lights from the pool. I watched him toss back the dregs of his tumbler then reach for Captain Morgan's. Instead of pouring it into a glass, he drank straight from the bottle, *glug, glug, glug,* until every last drop was gone. He then drew his arm slowly across his mouth before staring into the darkness.

We waited, listening to the sound of silence.

Three minutes later, J.J. closed his eyes, slid out of his chair and landed face down in the fescue. Despite numerous not so gentle pokes and prods, he wouldn't budge.

"Crap. How long before you think he wakes up?" Monica Lyn asked while prying open one of his eyelids and peering in.

"Dunno. He drank a lot. Could be a few hours, could be a few days."

"But you heard him, didn't you? He confessed to killing Kitty."

"You think the cops will take the word of two drunken women? Both of whom are prime suspects themselves?"

"Good point," Monica Lyn said. "One of us should have stayed sober."

"Us? Stay sober? Right." I tossed back the dregs of my drink. "So now what?" I asked, hoping home to bed was the answer.

Monica Lyn sat back in her chair and tapped her pointer finger against the enamel on her front tooth. I knew, having sat next to her for every test from third-grade spelling quizzes to high school calculus exams, finger tapping on a tooth meant she was deep in thought and shouldn't be interrupted.

"We need proof," she said. "And I've got an idea. A wonderful, awful idea." She sprang out of her chair, raced around the pool and disappeared into the house.

I waited for her return, watching J.J. sleep and wondering what had motivated him to kill Kitty. Especially in such a brutal way. They say everyone has a point that they will take another person's life, but rarely does one get pushed that far. What had been J.J.'s killing point?

Monica Lyn returned, wearing latex food preparation gloves and wielding a hacksaw and shovel. "Here, put these on," she said, tossing a pair of gloves in my direction. The shovel followed, landing with a thud at my feet. "Now go dig a hole by the back fence."

"What are you doing?" I asked as I watched her bend over J.J.'s body, hacksaw in hand.

"Putting his fingerprints on the saw that killed Kitty."

"OMG, you found the murder weapon?"

"Nope. No bloody saws hanging in the garage, so we're going to make this look like the murder weapon by covering it in J.J.'s prints then burying it in the backyard. Then we'll call in an anonymous tip to the police. They'll haul him in for questioning, and he'll confess under the pressure of the intense interrogation."

"How do you know he'll crack?"

"He always fidgeted when Beckett put the screws to someone on *Castle*. He'll crack faster than an egg dropped from a third-story window. I'll bet my life on it."

I donned the gloves, picked up the shovel and headed off towards the back fence to dig a hole. No doubt about it, Monica Lyn's had a criminal mind. I'm glad I was on her side.

* * * * * *

Damn Luminal," Monica Lyn said as she slammed her cell phone on the kitchen counter the next afternoon.

"What's that?" I asked while spreading strawberry preserves on my wheat toast. We'd been up for hours, but I was just getting around to breakfasting.

"It's a chemical agent that detects the presence of human blood. Even if the item has been washed, traces of iron remain and cast off a blue light when Luminal is sprayed on it."

"So?" I slipped along the bench seat the table, my mouth watering at the idea of tasting the homemade strawberry preserves. Monica Lyn's mother's preserves were the best on the planet, and I hadn't had any in years.

"So, no big surprise, there was no trace of blood on the hacksaw we buried in J.J.'s yard. Which means they can't tie J.J. to Kitty's murder. Which means he didn't even get hauled in for questioning. This also puts us back at the top of the list of suspects."

"Not us. You."

"You helped steal the trashcan and move the body."

I pushed my toast away and wondered how much jail time that might earn me.

"You heard him confess. He killed her, I know it. Sure as I know my own name. Which means the murder weapon is somewhere in that house. It's up to us to find it."

"How?" I don't know why I asked that, because I really didn't want to know the answer.

"I have a plan," Monica Lyn said. "Come on, best friend. Let's go."

Really, what choice did I have?

* * * * * *

Two days later, we returned to Monica Lyn's old house. J.J. was in Boston for the day, having "unexpectedly" received tickets to the Red Sox/Yankees game. Those tickets are hard to come by. Make that impossible. And I can't imagine what strings Monica Lyn had to pull to get a pair. But I didn't ask, and she didn't tell.

With the place to ourselves, we set out on a mission to find the murder weapon and/or the dismemberment tool. It's not like the police hadn't already searched the premises after our anonymous tip about the buried hacksaw, but we had the advantage in that Monica Lyn not only knew all the secret hidey-holes in the centuries-old mini-mansion, but also J.J.'s sneaky ways.

We started with the dusty attic and worked our way down to the musty basement. Nothing. I was starting to doubt that J.J. had done murder. And kind of/sort of, in the darkest recesses of my mind, began to wonder if Monica Lyn might not have been the one to have hit her killing point. That could explain her intense focus to frame J.J. in order to get away with it. It could explain her stumbling across the dead body in the first place. I mean, what are the odds that the one day she decides to steal J.J.'s trash can is the one day it's full of Kitty Kline's pieces parts? And now that I thought about it, she seemed a little too intent on proving J.J.'s guilt—and thus her innocence. Why not let the police work things out?

We'd finished our search of the garage and were heading along a cluttered breezeway/laundry room towards the house proper. "I need a drink," Monica Lyn said. "You?"

"Diet Coke." I followed her, my mind trying to hold back the questions leaking through the wall between conscious and subconscious thoughts. "With a splash of rum," I added, detouring to the half bath off to my left. "I'll be right there."

I closed the door and leaned against the pedestal sink, closing my eyes against the riotous jumble of tropical colors of the bathroom's décor. After drawing a deep breath of plumeria-scented bathroom air, I forced myself into a frank, honest, no-strings-of-friendship-attached assessment of the situation.

Monica Lyn hadn't taken J.J.'s infidelity well (what loving and devoted wife would, though?) nor were the divorce proceedings tilting at all in her favor. She was about to lose not only the man she loved and the house she'd turned into a home, but also the financial security she'd enjoyed all her adult life.

Maybe she'd gone to his house to try to work things out but found Kitty there alone, wearing the satin kimono Monica Lyn bought on their recent trip to Japan, or bathing in her Jacuzzi tub using her ME! Mulberry bath salts, or sitting around the pool drinking her Ketel vodka. That might have been enough to set Monica Lyn off. After all, Kitty was the cause of the unraveling marriage. (I'm not naïve enough to think that J.J. wouldn't have hooked up with Kitty had there not been other problems, but I'd only heard Monica Lyn's side of the story and the evidence was pretty damning against J.J.) Maybe, just maybe, an argument ensued and Monica Lyn reached her killing point.

After she'd killed Kitty and stuffed her in the Hefty Cinch-Saks, maybe Monica Lyn then concocted a plan to frame J.J. for the murder. My arrival in town cast me in the starring role of witness for the defense. I was the perfect shill. Innocent, trusting, faithful, and above all, in debt for a lifetime of favors.

There were a lot of maybes in there, but it all made perfect sense. Much more sense than all the other possibilities combined.

What would Monica Lyn do with me now that I'd figured it out? Would she blackmail me into keeping my mouth shut? Or would she make sure I kept my mouth shut by killing me too? Possibly. Wait, we're talking about Monica Lyn here. No "possibly" about it. Once Monica Lyn set a goal, there was not stopping her. And I was about to stop her from framing J.J. and pointing her out as a murderess.

A cold fear spread through my body. The type that set my teeth chattering. I had to get out of here. And I had to do it without Monica Lyn's knowledge or suspicion.

I reached for the doorknob, preparing to sneak out through the garage and down to the bus station. But the sound of angry voices coming from the kitchen gave me pause.

Monica Lyn's I identified, but the other I wasn't so sure about. It sounded like J.J., but the tone was lower and raspier. Maybe he'd caught a cold that night he'd slept poolside.

I opened the door a crack and saw Monica Lyn running down the breezeway, followed in hot pursuit by Scott Hunter, J.J.'s twin brother. The years had not been kind to the man. His once swarthy complexion was now ashy. His athlete's muscle had gone to fat. Those blue eyes, which had once sparkled with mischief, were nothing more than narrow slits of steel.

I watched as Scott reached out and grabbed Monica Lyn by the ponytail, snapping her head back. With a skill perfected by four years on the varsity wrestling team, he wrapped her in a full Nelson. And with just as much practiced ease, pressed a stiletto knife to her jugular. "You didn't fool me," Scott said, his voice sounding like sandpaper on granite, "sending J.J. off to the game so you could poke around his house and find evidence of his Ponzi scheme. The proceeds of which kept you living like the rich bitch you are."

"I don't care about his thieving ways. We were looking for the murder weapon, you jackass."

"J.J. didn't kill Kitty. I did," Scott boasted. "She found out about our little financial scheme and was threatening to go to the police. J.J. wouldn't last a day in prison. I'm just looking out for my bro'." Scott drew the knife slowly from the tip of Monica Lyn's hairline down her nose and across her chin.

Monica Lyn whimpered but didn't scream.

I almost screamed, but slapped my hands over my mouth to keep it in. It also helped keep in the vomit that bubbled up at the sight of the blood droplets forming along the slash line.

I eased back from the door and pressed my back against the cool tiles. *Think, think, THINK!* Scott was the killer, not J.J., not Monica Lyn. Of course not Monica Lyn. How foolish was I to think my best friend capable of such a heinous act?

If I didn't do something, Scott was going to slice and dice her, the way he had Kitty Kline. I couldn't hide in the bathroom while he did.

My eyes scanned the bathroom for some sort of weapon but found nothing heavier than a double role of Charmin.

Monica Lyn whimpered again.

I reached out and slid the medicine cabinet open. It contained one item, a bottle of OFF! bug spray. It wasn't much, but it was all I had.

Scott spoke again. "And now you're gonna join Kitty, the queen of sluts, at the bottom of the landfill. You and that sidekick of yours. Hey, where is Spring Roll, anyway?"

"She went to pick up lunch at Melba Moon's."

Now that was some BFF, trying to save me from being slashed up. How could I have ever doubted her?

"Good." Scott said. "I can take my time and enjoy this."

One heartbeat later, Monica Lyn let out a blood-curdling scream.

I didn't think, just acted.

With my eyes closed, I yanked open the door, leapt into the breezeway and pumped that bug spray with every ounce of self-preservation I had. A mixture of ethyl alcohol, DEET, aloe and fragrance filled the breezeway.

"Shit!" Scott yelled. "Shit! Shit! Shit!"

Sharp, slicing pain shot up my arm followed by spreading warmth that indicates a gushing blood flow. I directed my bottle of OFF! towards where I thought I heard Scott breathing, still pumping that plastic nozzle like my life depended on it. Which it did. I threw in a couple of swift kicks, making contact with something hard, but I didn't know if it was Scott or the washing machine, since my eyes remained closed. I kept spraying, moving my arm in sweeping arcs to make sure I covered all directions.

Silence registered on my senses. I cracked my peepers open just enough to scan the room. Scott was only a few inches away, rubbing his eyes with the palm of one hand, holding the knife in the other. Monica Lyn laid crumpled, facedown, on the ground, in a puddle of her own blood.

I reached for bottle of Clorox on the shelf near my elbow near and threw it at Scott. It glanced off his temple, knocking him backwards. In the process, he dropped the knife.

I pounced on that stiletto like a seagull on a bologna

sandwich, wrapping my hand around the hilt and slashing and stabbing in Scott's direction. He crab-crawled out of arm's reach, but I kept after him with sweeping slashing movements, not aiming, but hoping to make contact with a vital organ.

I heard the faint sounds of sirens in the distance. Monica Lyn must have had presence of mind to hit the panic button in the kitchen.

Scott must have heard them too, because he rolled to his hands and knees then to a sprinter's starting position.

I lunged forward, the Stiletto sinking deep into the back of his thigh.

"I'll kill you for that, bitch." Those were his parting words before he escaped out the garage door.

I ran to Monica Lyn's side and rolled her over. Gawd, it looked like he'd played a game of tick-tac-toe on her beautiful face. Her left eye dangled from its socket by the merest wisp of tissue. She'd lost a lot of blood, but was still breathing. Barely.

* * * * * *

Nothing would please me more than to report justice has been served and that Scott Hunter has been sent up the river for life without possibility of parole; that his twin-brother J.J. sailed with him for his knowledge of the murder; that Monica Lyn cleaned up in the divorce; and that I, as the hero of the day, returned to my quiet life as a cotton merchant in Memphis, Tennessee.

But things didn't turn out quite that way.

Scott escaped and was tracked as far as Nova Scotia, where he disappeared. He could be dead. Should be dead. Probably was dead. But there is the slim chance he is still alive and will someday track me down and finish the job of slicing me to pieces as promised.

J.J. was convicted of running a Ponzi scheme, the likes of which shook the small seaside town of Sagucci Bay to its core. But he had a good lawyer, and I'd lay even money he'd be out on parole in less than ten years.

Monica Lyn is scheduled for her third cosmetic surgery next week, but her beautiful face will never be the same. And it's not just physical pain she's suffering through, there's financial anguish, too. All those riches she and J.J. had enjoyed throughout their marital life went to payoff investors. No more McMansion on the hill. No more worldly travels. Not even any more ME! bath salts. She's moved in with her parents in their tiny house on Cottage Street.

As for me, I still have nightmares where Scott busts through my front door and slashes up more than my arm. The images haunt me during the waking hours, too. No longer able to keep my mind on task, I was fired from my job. I'm now working as a hostess at the Pig 'N Whistle until I am able to close that horrific chapter and move on with my life. It's going to take time, though.

My happy, carefree evenings filled with "Seas the Day" toasts are gone.

Right now, I can't go five minutes without looking down at my arm. Every time I do, my finger traces the pink scar that runs from my wrist to my elbow, a forever reminder of when I'd been middle aged and foolish.

And brave.

THE END

THE TIDE ALSO RISES

"The Tide Also Rises" shares the escapades of Dee Dee Nesbitt, who is house sitting at her best friend's recently inherited house on the Chesapeake Bay. Her responsibilities include lounging on the back deck while egrets fly overhead, and the care and feeding of baby oysters. All is not well in this coastal paradise, however, after a dead body floats in on the tide.

THE TIDE ALSO RISES

Noisy buggars, ain't they?" The too-much-whiskey-and-cigarettes voice of my new neighbor startled me. I thought I was alone in my bungling efforts to haul what seemed like twelve miles of green hose from the house, across the two acres of lawn, and down the high-above-the-marsh-grass dock.

One dock over, Mrs. McAlistair stared at me from her Adirondack chair. Her beady eyes made me feel guilty. For what, I hadn't a clue.

"Huh?" I grunted. I hated it when my student's "huh"-ed me, but the 102-degree heat combined with physical efforts of a body trained in more leisurely pursuits—like lounging in the hammock while losing myself in a sizzling romance—had made me grumpy. I resented being watched. True southern manners required an offer of assistance. I now understood what Cherise had meant when she'd whispered to me, "Watch out for Mrs. McAllister. She's a Yank."

"The egrets," Mrs. McAlister said, nodding in the direction of a large white, dangly-legged bird soaring overhead. "Noisy buggars."

The shore birds screeched in a way that sounded like a woman being strangled. "Oh, yeah. Took some getting used to." I continued my heaving and hoeing of the hose, needing at least another ten feet to reach the end of the dock. Despite my best efforts, the rubber tube wouldn't budge. Ironically, I thought I'd got the best end of the deal when my friend had offered me two months rent-free at her recently inherited *Coastal Living*-inspired home overlooking the marshes of Beacon's Creek and the Chesapeake Bay beyond. In exchange, I'd be responsible for caring for the oysters growing in a mesh bag hanging off the dock. All that was required was a weekly hosing off. It had sounded simple enough, but right now, I was thinking I'd been hoodwinked. Some things looked better on paper.

The foster oyster program is part of the Save the Chesapeake Bay project. The "Tschiswapeki", as the Native Americans called it, meant "Great Shellfish Bay." But 20th-century over-harvesting, disease and pollution has reduced the population by more than ninety-nine percent. With each oyster filtering fifty gallons of water per day and their numbers so greatly reduced, it didn't take a nuclear physicist to figure out the bay was in need of life support.

Part of the solution is repopulating the oysters. People like my friend Cherise do their part by raising pea-sized infants to baseball-sized adolescence. The spat, as baby oysters are called, are corralled in a mesh bag settled in a large PVC-pipe-and-wire nest floating off the end of their dock. After a year of care, the oysters are loaded onto a skiff and sent out to the bay. With a ceremonious splash, they are dumped overboard to start a new oyster reef. The little shellfish get busy filtering, and the bay's health improves. Marginally. It's a very small piece in a very large, problematic puzzle.

Cherise was to be commended for her role in it. Only she bailed when an opportunity to fulfill a lifelong dream came along—a summer course in petit fours at *Le Cordon Bleu*. This, in turn, enabled me to fulfill my lifelong dream of a summer spent along the shore. My only responsibilities were the bi-weekly rinsing of mud off the mesh bag, and plucking out fiddler crabs that had bellied up to an all-you-can-eat oyster buffet. Like I said, some things look better on paper.

After wiping my hands on my T-shirt, I grabbed the

hose and gave it one hard tug. It didn't budge. Experienced hose wrangler I'm not, but common sense told me it must have snagged on something, because Cherise had assured me the house hose would reach the dock.

I didn't relish the idea of the long trek back to the house, especially in the three-inch strappy sandals that had looked like perfect by-the-sea attire when I'd spotted them in the store window. I sighed and did what any blue-blooded southern girl who didn't want to sweat would do—I grabbed the hose tight and yanked for all I was worth.

The hose unengaged.

I stumbled backwards.

My heel caught between two boards.

I fell with a splash into Beacon's Creek.

It being low tide and all, it was more of Beacon's Mud Flats and I ended up with mud in places a lady doesn't discuss in polite company.

And to make my embarrassment complete, Mrs. McAllister was laughing her ass off.

I wanted to scream.

And then I did, when I realized that what I thought was stick tangled in my hair was really the hand of a dead man.

* * * * * *

Shock is a funny thing. Despite the sizzling temperature, I shivered like a pair of cheesy wind-up teeth under Mrs. McAlister's tattered quilt. It wasn't so much the sucking sound of the mud wanting to keep its treasure as the police pulled the body from the water. Nor the front row seat as they stretched the bloated, lifeless, crab-picked body on the dock. Not even the wiping of mud from the victim's face and proclaiming, "It's Elliott King," before covering him with a tarp. No, my shock had its roots in the repetitive and accusatory tone of the detective's questions. And I didn't find his crooked ball cap imprinted with "Guilty

Until Proven Innocent" the least bit amusing. Granted, he'd been called in from a fishing trip with his son and hadn't had time to change clothes, but how hard would it have been to switch into his professional ball cap?

"Do you need anything?" asked the freckle-faced young cop assigned to making sure I didn't run screaming for the hills. Officer Grady, according to his name badge.

"Yeah. A glass of pinot noir would be great. Pantry next to the fridge. Second shelf." I looked at him and he looked at me—that same you-did-it stare that I'd suffered under too often today. "On second thought, make it a double."

"There's a program for that," he said to me, sliding his hands along his utility belt until his right one settled on the butt of his gun. "Called AA. They meet every Thursday in the basement of the First Presby—"

"I'm not an alcoholic, you idiot." The fact that I'd insulted one of Beacon's Creek's finest was proof that I wasn't in my right mind. I took a deep breath.

"That's not what Mizz. McAlister told us."

"What does that crazy old busybody know? I've never said more than a dozen words to her." Not civil words, anyway. I wasn't counting the profanity that had spewed from the darkest recesses of my mind when I'd found that body and she'd taken her sweet time calling 911.

"Mizz. McAlister makes it her business to know everything that's going on along the creek."

"Sounds like somebody should remind Mrs. McAlister that curiosity killed the cat. Now how about that wine?"

"You can't drink away—"

"Listen. I'm covered in mud and smell like dead fish. I've shark rolled with a dead man, and donated my brand-new shoes to the creek. Now I need a small glass of wine." The officer stared at me. "Now!" I used my sternest teacher voice, which garnered the required action. He'd probably get busted to meter maid when his sergeant found out he was playing wine steward, but my nerves were wound like a Slinky and needed some serious un-kinking.

Officer Grady returned minutes later with an iced-tea glass filled to the rim with ruby red liquid. I settled back in the hammock and took a long sip. Well, *Webster's* would probably define it a gulp. My gaze skipped over the disapproving eyes of the officer and out over the marsh. "You say he's a local boy?" I asked.

"Yes'um. Scotty King's eldest. Moved to Hot-lanta about three months ago. His momma held a big shindig in the basement of the First Presbyterian Church the night 'fore he left. Must a' been over a hundred people there. Real nice party. Catered 'n everything." Officer O'Grady smacked his lips as if he'd just finished gnawing on a turkey leg.

"Any guess as to how he died?" I took another gulp, then swirled the glass and watched the wine ebb and flow. A small amount dribbled over the rim, and I licked it the way I would have a melting ice cream cone.

"I'm not a forensics expert, but I'd say the bullet through his heart's prob'ly what done him in."

"Yeah. That's usually an effective way to make sure somebody never sees another sunrise."

The gurney laden with a tarp-covered body rolled within five feet of where I sat. That image, the sounds of the creaky conveyance, the smell of brackish water and rotting flesh, would haunt my dreams for the rest of my life.

* * * * * *

Funerals are funny things. At least Mrs. McAlister seemed to think so. She sat next to me, snorting and guffawing like we were front at center at the Comedy Club. Granted, Reverend Hanna's overly dramatic reading of "Crossing the Bar" was worthy of an eye roll, but not side-splitting hysterics. I gave her a sharp elbow in the ribs. "Hush, now," I hissed through clenched teeth.

"Oh, hush yourself," she said in what we in the teaching world call an outside voice. And she sure could throw a mean elbow for such a feeble-looking seasoned citizen.

I massaged my side and slunk lower in my seat, ignoring the disapproving glares of those around us. I regretted accepting my nosy neighbor's invitation to accompany her to the funeral. She'd said it would be therapeutic and put an end to my nightmares. I was beginning to think spending the afternoon in her company might spark worse ones. "I don't see what's the least bit funny about Elliott's death," I hissed back.

She leaned in close, her raspy voice tickling my ear. "It's not his death that I'm laughing at, but the hypocrites sitting here pretending they care he's gone. I guarantee you more than half are here because they think the killer is among the ranks and they want to be able to brag they rubbed elbows with a murderer." Her gaze darted around the room then back at me. "And I know for a fact every single person is here for the fried chicken dinner in the basement that follows the service. Elliott's Memaw hired The Gravy Train to cater." Mrs. McAlister settled back in the pew. A Mona Lisa-like smile worked its way across her wrinkled, weathered skin. She'd probably been quite a looker in her youth, what with those high cheekbones and perky nose, but the years had not been all that kind to her.

I thought about what she'd said, and my head went all tingly, like somebody was rolling a piecrust crimper from the base of my skull all the way over the top of my head. Could the killer really be among us?

* * * * * *

It takes three things to prove murder in a court of law." Mrs. McAlister continued her short course in Murder Investigation 101.

My mind wasn't on the murder. It was on licking the chicken grease from my fingers. To. Die. For. And the pineapple coleslaw? Words cannot express my gastronomic pleasure. I shoveled another forkful into my not-quite-empty mouth. Three more bites and I'd be an official member of the clean-plate club, with just enough room left in my stomach for a generous helping of warm peach cobbler and cold vanilla ice cream. *Mmm mmm mmm.*

"Way I see it, you have means and opportunity, but I'm having trouble with the motive," Mrs. McAlister said.

I choked.

Mrs. McAlister smacked me on the back so hard I hocked up food I'd eaten two days ago. I sputtered and coughed and wheezed and gasped. Finally I managed a coherent defense. "Me?"

"The police chief told me this morning that Elliott'd been lying in the mud for two weeks."

"So?"

"You've been living at the Montague place for two weeks."

"So?"

"Body found at the end of the dock."

"So?"

"I've seen you out on the dock."

"So?"

"You have experience with guns."

I felt the blood drain from my face. "How . . ."

Mona Lisa smiled again before speaking. "Cherise bragged on you. Wanna tell me about it?"

"Nope." My gaze dropped to my plate of food, and I pushed it away. My taste for peach cobbler was replaced by a churning of gruesome memories. Blood. Intestines. The smell of death. A terrible, horrific accident our senior year in high school. Cherise and I had both been dumped by our boyfriends and drowned our sorrows in mango margaritas. Getting tattoos seemed like the greatest idea in the world. While we stumbled along the sleazy side of town in search of a tattoo parlor, a young kid jumped us from behind and held a gun to Cherise's head. She kicked him where it counts and he dropped the gun. I grabbed it. He pulled a knife. I pulled the trigger. The way Cherise tells it, I saved her life. From my perspective, I killed another human being.

Fighting the bile gurgling beneath my tonsils, I excused myself and went to the ladies' room. Cold water to my wrists and cheeks calmed me a bit, but my legs still felt like wet noodles. I collapsed onto the green velveteen chaise lounge and allowed myself a moment of self-pity. Mrs. McAlister seemed hell bent on pinning Elliott's murder on me. The only question was, why?

* * * * * *

Dusk had settled into a magnetic blue by the time I emerged from the First Presbyterian Church. I scanned the parking lot but saw no sign of Mrs. McAlister's ghost-gray Beemer. That suited me fine, because I really didn't want to ride in a car with someone who thought I went around killing people.

Cherise's house was three miles outside of town, down a sparsely-populated road. My feet had protested when I'd squeezed them into the two-sizes-too-small, three-inch heels (that had been too cute and too price-reduced to pass up), and they weren't at all happy with the prospect of walking that far. I had a personal paradigm not to ride with strangers when I was alone, especially out here where I didn't know a soul. Way I figured it, I had two options: call Mrs. McAlister and beg her to come get me; hitch a ride with a stranger; or take my shoes off and hoof it to my temporary digs. It was such a beautiful night, I chose option B, and headed south along the sand- and sea-oats-lined road.

My time in the ladies' room had proved fruitful. I'd overheard enough conversations to understand the number one suspect in Elliott's murder was not me, thankfully, but a guy named Scary Jerry. Associated with drugs, gambling, and prostitution in the area, he was not exactly a pillar of the community. Current conjecture was Elliott had tried to nose in on Scary Jerry's turf. Elliott's relocation to Atlanta was to be a fresh start for him. So how had he ended back in Beacon's Creek? And dead, at that?

Scary Jerry had motive, and I'm guessing means, since carrying a gun was probably a job requirement in his line of work. All that was left to earn a conviction was opportunity. I allowed myself a Walter Mitty-type fantasy of solving the murder myself. Concluding, of course, with a nose thumbing at my neighbor when I accepted an honorarium from the police chief.

The sound of a diesel engine jarred me from my thoughts. Headlights swept across my path, and I stepped off the road to wait for it to pass. Instead, a red pick-'em-up truck slowed down and pulled off the road, the tires rolling within inches of my toes.

"Need a lift little lady?"

My feet screamed YES. They hurt beyond belief.

My heart screamed YES. It was getting dark, and strange noises echoed from the untamed fields leading down to the shore.

My brain, however, was not so quick to agree. I'd had a life-threatening experience in a big-city taxi a few years ago. I'd had to jump out of the taxi when it slowed down to make a turn. Broke my wrist, but lived to tell the story. Hence my policy not to ride with strangers. Ever.

Until now.

I could keep walking for another hour at the risk of a million bug bites and a possible close encounter of the coyote kind (I'd read about that very issue in the paper last week.) Or I could accept a ride and in five minutes be on Cherise's back porch, curled up with a book and a glass of pinot noir.

I made a quick mental inventory of the truck's driver. Dark suit, Curly graying hair. Crooked smile. Dumbo-sized ears. I remembered him from the funeral, so he wasn't a complete stranger. And a point in his favor is he reminded me of Andy Griffith, the sheriff who never carried a gun. He seemed harmless, and I've always been a good judge of character.

"That would be great." I opened the door and tossed my shoes on the red vinyl seat before climbing in myself. "I should probably trade in my stilettos for flip flops if I'm going to be hiking around here." I slammed the truck door behind me and relaxed against the seat. My feet felt happier already.

Too much gas without sufficient release of the clutch had the engine roaring and the gravel spinning. I grabbed the "Oh Shit" handle over my head and held on for all I was worth.

"You're McAlister's new neighbor, ain'tchye?"

It occurred to me my driver's speech was slurred. And he was having trouble staying between the lines on the road.

"Ma name's Jerry."

As in Scary Jerry?

My stomach dropped as if an elevator had plummeted seventy-five stories. Jerry's a common enough name, I reminded myself. There had to be more than one in town. "Nice to meet you." My voice sounded light, and I hoped carefree. Two summers at drama camp were paying off. "I'm house sitting for my friend Cherise. She's in France. In cooking school. Something she's wanted to do since she was a little girl." In this small town, I suspected he knew that already, but I always babble to cover my nervousness. And riding shotgun with a drunk driver who might—or might not, I hoped—be a killer made me more nervous than I had ever been in my entire life. That included the night we'd been attacked on our way to get tattoos.

We cruised through a stop sign while driving on the wrong side of the road and I slipped my hand down and wrapped it around the cool metal of the door handle. At the first sign of speeds below 20 mph, I planned to roll out. I figured my odds of surviving were better out of the truck than in.

"Nice place Cherise got up 'chere. What luck her uncle kicked the bucket. But he had a bit a help, if you know what ah mean."

No, I didn't know what he meant at all. Cherise hadn't said much about her uncle's *modus moriendi*.

I had a super sick feeling in the pit of my stomach. And it wasn't from bad chicken or swervy driving. "Uh . . ." I cleared the gravel from my throat. "Umm, what makes you think it wasn't an accident?" It occurred to me I didn't really want to know the answer, because people who have knowledge of how others were murdered often ended up dead themselves.

"That's something for Whitchy McAlister ta know 'n' for you ta find out."

The truck skittered to a stop, taking Cherise's mailbox with it. I slammed my shoulder against the truck door, and then slipped to safety. "Thanks," I called to the taillights fading into the darkness, and the illuminated license plate that said SCRYJRY. "I think."

* * * * * *

Armed with a goblet of a playful Beaujolais, I began a search for anything and everything I could learn about Cherise's Uncle Henry's death. I had a freaky feeling his and Elliott's untimely demises were intricately entwined. And an even freakier feeling that Scary Jerry was the missing link.

An Internet search provided me the basics. Henry Wilson Montague had made his millions in plastics. While reaching the pinnacle of financial success, Henry's life was a lesson in money not being able to buy happiness. He married young, but lost his wife soon after when she died giving birth to their only child, Lilibeth. She'd died at the ripe old age of seventeen in what was hinted as a tragic accident but no details forthcoming, at least not that I could find.

Henry had retired one month before his death and settled into this coastal retreat I now occupied. There was no indication as to his connection to this sparsely populated area along the shore. No family ties, no water-related hobbies, no nearby cultural attractions that often drew the retired set. He could have lived anywhere in the world, so why here? Granted, the scenic vistas of sun setting on the creek soothed the aching soul, and fresh air and solitude were appealing. Perhaps that's what he needed?

His short-lived retirement ended when he suffered a heart attack while driving to the grocery store. He'd slammed into a speeding semi-truck. No mention of him taking anyone else to heaven with him, thank God.

What did Jerry know that the medical examiner didn't?

A through search of rooms, closets, files, medicine cabinets, and storage bins revealed no trace of Henry's habitation. In the four months Cherise had lived here, she'd successfully de-uncled the place. Not so much as a picture or piece of mail with his name on it.

I felt rather than saw dawn sneak over the horizon. A new day. Despite my fatigue, I was determined to push onward. I only had the attic to search. Then I could sleep.

I dragged my tired body up the attic stairs, where over a hundred boxes awaited me. A quick glance confirmed they were all neatly labeled "HM's stuff." Now, why hadn't I begun my search here?

Where to begin? There was no marking that said "Look here for the clue to the murders." The only thing to do was go through them box by box by box. Fortified with two liter of Diet Coke and a sleeve of Fig Newtons, I set to work.

The first thing I learned about Henry Montague was that he was a pack rat. I'd never seen so much junk in my life. Dating way back to his childhood, there were thousands of moldy, mildew-y mementoes that set me to sneezing with each opened box.

The second thing I learned was that Henry had not always been honest in his business dealings. Seven boxes of legal suits and counter suits accused him of everything from fraud to intellectual property theft. I thought I'd hit pay dirt when I found an entire folder of death threats, but the dates were when Scary Jerry would have been playing with plastic guns.

My head felt like a bowling ball and the front of my T-shirt was soaked through with nasal drainage in response to the dust and mold heavy in the attic. I craved fresh air, food and sleep, but not necessarily in that order. Time for a break.

I'd worked my way about two-thirds of the way across the attic, but had kind of boxed myself in in the process. I'd moved opened boxes behind me as I worked my way deeper into the attic. When it came time to retreat, I climbed my way across the room, schootching around and over opened boxes. Slow going, to be sure.

Almost there, but I misjudged my step and fell against a stack of boxes, toppling them over. In true Murphy's-Law fashion, the contents splattered out over the floor and down the steps. Pencils, papers, framed awards with glass now shattered, now lay scattered at my feet. But there was also something I hadn't noticed on my original search . . . a red satin journal. An odd choice for a man, to be sure. I fanned the pages to find the journal almost two-thirds full of flowing script that practically screamed of female penmanship.

More curious than ever, I tucked the journal under my arm, tip-toed my way around the boxes' detritus, and made my way downstairs. This journal needed to be read, and it needed to be read now.

Armed with more caffeine and more snacks (Pringles this time—I was on vacation, after all), I headed out into the sunshine. The heatwave had passed, and the morning bordered on cool, at least by southeast Virginia standards. The hammock, stretched between two gloriously green maple trees, called to me. I answered. The ropes cradled me as I fed my hunger and curiosity with equal enthusiasm.

Lilibeth--the Teenage Years did not disappoint.

* * * * * *

I followed the emotional rollercoaster of Henry's daughter from the age of fifteen (when she defied her father and snuck out to meet a bad boy named Willie) through her seventeenth birthday. The drama played out through the very last entry:

Daddy gave MY earrings to Miriam. The ones he'd promised would be MINE on my 18th birthday. I want to kill him. And I will. And I'll make Miriam watch and then I'll kill her, too. A slow and painful death. And she'll beg me to stop. And she'll cry and tell me how she never wanted those old earrings anyway, even if they were a gift to my grandma from a crowned prince. She'll try to convince me I have the perfect coloring for emeralds. That I deserve them and she'd never be worthy. Never. I'll laugh and dangle them in her face as she takes her last breath . . .

Only in Hollywood would the girl have faked her own death and waited 50 years to fulfill her vow to kill her father. Dead end.

Despite hours of searching, I was no closer to unearthing Henry's killer that I had been last night.

Needing something physical to do to keep awake, I decided to give the oysters their overdue bath. I hadn't ventured back onto the pier since the discovery of Elliot's body four days ago. And if I thought about it very long, I'd talk myself out of it again today.

I marched to the corner of the garage, grabbed the end of the hose and dragged it across the yard and down to the dock. The creek circled and swirled as it ebbed back to sea. Tides run on a twelve and a half-hour cycle, which doesn't match up to a twenty-four-hour world. That means each high and low tide occurs thirty minutes later each day. That had me wondering where in the tide cycle Elliott's body had been dumped. If it had been me, I'd have tossed it at ebb tide so the body would be carried out to the bay, never to be found. A flood tide would carry it up the creek, where the water became increasingly shallow and increasingly likely to be discovered. Maybe Elliot's body had been tossed into the middle of the bay and the tide had carried it to this dock? Maybe the killer hadn't been a waterman, hadn't known that summer tides aren't as high as winter tides? Maybe the body had been buried in the mud, and only through my clumsiness had been uncovered?

I shrugged off the feeling of a ghost walking across my grave as my gaze swept across the marsh grass. A lone, long-legged egret stood above the shallow water, not moving. Waiting, waiting, waiting for his breakfast to come to him. Fast as lightening, its head jerked beneath the surface and emerged clutching a silver fish. Massive wings spread out and the bird flew elsewhere to enjoy its breakfast.

The facts of the murders swirled with the vision of the dangly legged egret and my visualization of Lilibeth's dangly emerald earrings. Faces swam before me: from the funeral, from the newspaper clippings, from Henry's photo albums. I started to add two plus two but no matter how I ciphered, I came up with six.

Soft footsteps scratched along the dock. I turned. Great. The last person I wanted to see. Mrs. McAlister. And I doubly didn't want to see her when I saw what was in her hands. In one, she clutched the red satin diary. In the other, a menacing handgun.

My heart stopped beating, my lungs stopped respirating. The only autonomic response working on me right now were my sweat glands. It felt like Niagara Falls rushing under my arms.

"So, you figured it all out?" Her raspy voice had me wanting to clear my throat.

"Huh?"

She wiggled the red diary. She waggled the gun.

The jumble of thoughts in my head came together in a flash of clarity. At the funeral, Mrs. McAlister had worn emerald earrings. She was a Yank. Henry's business had been based near Cleveland, Ohio. All thoughts led to Mrs. McAlister having killed Lilibeth over the earrings. "Why kill Henry after all these years?" The sound of my voice startled me. I hadn't meant to speak my thoughts aloud.

"He retired. Found the diary. Read it. Of course, I denied it when he accused me. He didn't believe me, but he didn't have any proof. He moved here to make what's left of my life a guilty hell."

"And Elliot?"

"Because he'd done my dirty work slipping some oleander to Henry so he'd have a heart attack. After that, he started blackmailing me for more money."

"So, you killed Elliott and were trying to frame me." No question. Just a statement of fact.

"Yup. I couldn't believe my luck. Of course, it wasn't lucky the body washed up, but you were an easy mark to take the fall."

Miriam McAlister aimed the gun at my heart and pulled the trigger.

* * * * * *

The beeping of a heartbeat monitor woke me from a deep sleep. My eyes fluttered open and the sweet face of my best friend Cherise stared down at me. "Took the red-eye back from Paris as soon as they called me."

"Hurts . . ." One word took all my strength.

Cherise patted my hand. "Of course it does."

"What . . ." More words were too difficult. I glanced at all the machines and Cherise got my message.

"Little gunshot wound to your shoulder. Knocked yourself out hitting the dock. Little bit of creek water in your lungs, but nothing some strong antibiotics won't knock out. You've been in a medically induced coma for two days. I wasn't sure you'd ever wake up. I'd better ring for a nurse."

I held on to her hand, not letting her move away while I processed that information. Still a lot of questions. I needed answers before the medical team started their poking and prodding. "How?" I managed to squeak out.

"How did you get shot?"

I shook my head, but that slight movement sent pain shooting down the back of my neck and settled between my shoulder blades. I took a deep breath and managed to move my lips while I exhaled. "How did I get here?" I whispered.

"Oh, that. Officer O'Grady happened to be walking across the lawn. He'd come to arrest you for Elliott's murder. He saw Mrs. McAlister pull a gun out and shoot you. He jumped in the creek and pulled you out."

"Saved my life."

"Yes, he did." Cherise's voice quavered a bit. "And I will be forever grateful for that." She rubbed my arm, a bit aggressively, but I knew the action was fueled by emotion. "You're coming to live with me until you are completely healed. Even if that takes the rest of the century."

I blinked my appreciation of the offer. But it wouldn't be very recuperative living next to the woman who tried to kill me. "Ms. McAlister?"

"Admitted to killing Elliott and Uncle Henry. And also my cousin Lilibeth, whom I obviously never met."

"How?"

"Made it look like suicide by hanging."

How tragic for Henry. A lot of heartache in his life. And just when he was about to exact some revenge, he ended up dead, too.

I, on the other hand, seemed to be one lucky woman to have survived being shot at close range. Even luckier that a police officer was there to catch the killer. And save my life.

I had a long road of recovery ahead of me, I knew. But I also believed the cure for everything was saltwater, be it sweat, tears or the sea. I expected in my case it is gonna take all three.

THE END

ABOUT THE AUTHOR

JAYNE ORMEROD writes what she knows—small towns (influenced by her childhood growing up in Chagrin Falls, Ohio) and beach settings (a result of 30 years as a navy spouse, always living within a flip-flop's throw of the ocean.) Thanks to a youth spent reading Nancy Drew and an adulthood devouring the words of Janet Evanovich, Mary Daheim and Lillian Jackson Braun, she can now write about amateur sleuths, exploding cars and dead bodies with a modicum of authority.

Raised in a 150-year old farmhouse, Jayne honed her story-telling skills at a tender age, convincing herself and others her home was haunted. She wove epic sagas of buried treasure guarded by spirits of slain pirates, and the soul of a crazed aunt locked in the attic, pacing the floorboards for all eternity. It wasn't until Jayne grew up that she learned of the dwelling's illustrious past as a house of ill repute. Oh, how much more, ah, colorful her ghost stories could have been.

Many moves (19 for anyone counting...) in conjunction with her husband's service in the U.S. Navy did not accommodate Jayne's blossoming career as a CIA (not the sexy "secret agent" kind, but a Certified Internal Auditor). She needed something more transportable. Thus, Jayne began her new writing career penning romance novels. She soon learned attempting to keep two desperately in love people at odds with each other for 300 pages was harder than it looked. The experience caused her to overdose on chocolate.

It was a childhood love of Nancy Drew books that sparked Jayne's dream of writing cozy mystery stories. Much like the Intrepid Girl Detective, each of Jayne's stories feature a female amateur sleuth, and there is always an element of danger. Most have an element of humor woven through. All are lighthearted in tone and sprinkled with enough clues that the reader should be able to solve the crime along with the character.

To learn more about Jayne (like why she uses a *nom de plume*) and to keep abreast of her latest releases, visit her website at www.JayneOrmerod.com. To further connect with Jayne and her writings, click on over to her Life's a Beach blog at www.JayneOrmerod.blogspot.com Social media? Yes, she's on Facebook as Jayne Ormerod, Author. But she limits her time on social media in order to focus on developing more great cozy adventure stories for her dedicated readers.

THE COMPLETE LIST OF PUBLISHED WORKS

of Cozy Mystery Writer

JAYNE ORMEROD

More info at www.JayneOrmerod.com

BLOND FAITH
A Blonds at the Beach Mystery

With 31,536,000 seconds in a year, what are the odds that the one minute Ellery Tinsdale and Samantha "Sam" Greene choose to break into the confidential files at the Braddocks Beach Church of Divine Spiritual Enlightenment would be the same minute Reverend John Thomas Hammersmith is brutally murdered while eating lunch at his desk? But that's the kind of bad luck Ellery experiences since moving to the small lakeside resort founded by her distant relatives. Her and Sam's close proximity to the tragic event makes them not only witnesses but suspects, too. And when not one, but two, more residents are found dead, Ellery and Sam are the unlucky ones to discover those bodies as well. Police Chief Lewis thinks it is more than a coincidence, and it's up to Ellery and Sam to clear their names by finding the killer—or killers—roaming the streets of this small Ohio town.

THE BLOND LEADING THE BLOND
A Blonds at the Beach Mystery

Ellery Tinsdale's father never talked about his childhood, never once mentioned what happened to his family, and never ever gave any indication there existed a lakefront resort in central Ohio founded by his ancestors. Curious upon receiving notice of the death of an aunt she hadn't known existed, Ellery travels to Braddocks Beach in hopes of learning a bit about her heritage. There she finds she is to inherit the family house, the family jewels, the family real estate holdings, the family bank accounts, and, much to her dismay, the family role of Queen Bee. Ellery also finds herself accused of Aunt Izzy's murder.

Samantha Greene is the lifelong friend and neighbor of Isabel Tinsdale, as well as the self-appointed purveyor of Braddocks Beach history. The recent discovery of a surviving member of Braddocks Beach's 'royal family' sets the town abuzz with anticipation of Ellery's arrival. But Sam soon learns that Ellery is the only person to ever flunk out of Madame Rowena's School of Etiquette and has much to learn about making appearances, leading charity drives, heading up committees, and setting fashion trends. But first and foremost is the business of clearing the Tinsdale name of murder.

What do a third-grade science teacher and a small-town socialite know about tracking killers? It's what they don't know that may hurt them.

TO FETCH A THIEF
Four Fun "Tails" of Theft and Murder . . .

This is the first book in the Mutt Mysteries series and is comprised of four novellas that have gone to the dogs. In this howling good read, canine companions help their owners solve crimes and right wrongs. These sleuths may be furry and low to the ground, but their keen senses are on high alert when it comes to sniffing out clues and digging up the truth. Make no bones about it, these pup heroes will steal your heart as they conquer *ruff* villains.

In Jayne's story, "It's a Dog Gone Shame!", Meg Gordon and her tawny terrier Cannoli are hot on the trail of a thief, a heartless one who steals rocks commemorating neighborhood dogs who have crossed the Rainbow Bridge. But sniffing out clues leads them to something even more merciless. . . a dead body! There's danger afoot as the two become entangled in the criminality infesting their small bayside community. It's a doggone shame, and Meg is determined to get to the bottom of things.

50 SHADES OF CABERNET
A Mysterious Anthology

In vino mysterium is the theme for this anthology of short stories, each blending a baffling mystery and a glass (or more) of cabernet. When eighteen mystery writers combine their talents, the result is the perfect "flight" of stories that range from light-bodied puzzles to sparkling cozies to darker, heavier tales of deceit and murder. While cabernet is the featured wine, this anthology will appeal to connoisseurs of all varietals--in both wine preference and mystery style.

This anthology includes Jayne's short mystery, "Life is a Cabernet". Here's the tease: Randa Miller has been lured to the Mahjongg Maniacs convention by the promise of wine. Thankfully, there is plenty of it, as she's found it's the only thing that can calm her nerves after discovering a dead body.

VIRGINIA IS FOR MYSTERIES
Volume 2

Virginia may be for lovers, but to nineteen authors, Virginia is for More Mysteries. The anthology of nineteen short stories, set in and around the Commonwealth, features Virginia landmarks and locations such as Virginia Wine Country, Poe Museum, Luray Caverns, Colonial Williamsburg, Great Dismal Swamp, Nimrod Hall, Barter Theater, and Mill Mountain, to name a few. The stories transport readers across the diverse backdrop of the Old Dominion to a unique and deadly landscape, filled with killers, crooks, and criminals. (Sisters in Crime).

"It's Wine o'Clock Somewhere" is Jayne's contribution. Set in Yorktown, VA, the story is summarized as follows: Real estate agents see a lot of things in the houses they tour, but a bomb shelter with a dead body is a first for Terri Sullivan. The only way to clear her name and get her clients back after becoming a suspect is to find the real killer herself.

VIRGINIA IS FOR MYSTERIES

Yes, Virginia may be for lovers, but it's for mysteries, too. At least according to 14 writers from the Old Dominion. *Virginia Is for Mysteries* is a collection of seventeen short stories set in and around the state of Virginia. All stories are written by Virginia residents with "murder" in mind. Each story features a Virginia landmark—from the shores of Cape Henry Lighthouse to Richmond's Old Hollywood Cemetery to Jefferson's Monticello—and transports readers across Virginia's rich, unique, and very deadly landscape.

This anthology includes Jayne's short humorous mystery, "Best Friends Help You Move the Body." Here's the pitch: "Playing hooky from work lands two best friends in trouble when their day of sightseeing has them discovering only one thing...a dead body."

BY THE BAY 2
More East Beach Stories

The East Beach writers are at it again, this time offering 14 new fictional tales about life along the Chesapeake Bay. The neighborhood of East Beach in Norfolk, Virginia, is the setting for these vignettes of family, friendship, mystery, history, adventure, love, and light-hearted fun. Join the characters as they walk the tree-lined streets, stroll the sandy shores, or relax on a rocking chair on one of the deep front porches that define this community.

This anthology includes Jayne's shorty mystery, "Write by the Bay". About the story: Carrie Hanover solves mysteries--in the literary sense. She's a writer. But when valuable jewels go missing from her landlady's home, Carrie finds herself embroiled in a real mystery . . . one fraught with real danger.

BY THE BAY
East Beach Stories
A collection of twelve fictional tales about life along the Chesapeake Bay, they range from murderous to romantic, from humorous to dramatic, from gritty noir to political thriller to the sweet and the spiritual. The thread that ties them together is their connection to a 100-acre peninsula in Norfolk, Virginia. East Beach is nestled on the shores of the southernmost point of the Chesapeake Bay, just as it becomes the Atlantic Ocean. Written by members of the East Beach Writers Guild, these tales exhibit the writers' love of their neighborhood and their talent for story-telling. All proceeds from the sales of these books will be disbursed to reading-related non-profits in the Norfolk, Virginia area.

Jayne has two stories in the anthology:

"Secrets" There are no secrets that time doesn't reveal... That's a line from a movie that earned Stella Gardner her first Oscar. Stella's own secrets harken back to her youth growing up on the eastern peninsula Norfolk, now known as East Beach.

"The Sniper Sisters" East Beach residents Dorothy Westmoreland and her sister Evelyn Binghamton have retired from lives of organizing bake sales and attending civic league meetings. But that doesn't mean they're sitting in their rocking chairs. No, not these two. They become active in their community . . . in a way nobody expects.